WHERE
PEOPLE
LIKE US
LIVE

WHERE PEOPLE LIKE US LIVE

Patricia Cumbie

LAURA GERINGER BOOKS
HARPER TEEN
An Imprint of HarperCollins*Publishers*

HarperTeen is an imprint of HarperCollins Publishers.

Where People Like Us Live
Copyright © 2008 by Patricia Cumbie

Library of Congress Cataloging-in-Publication Data
Cumbie, Patricia.
    Where people like us live / by Patricia Cumbie. — 1st ed.
        p.   cm.
    Summary: When her restless family moves to Racine, Wisconsin, fourteen-year-old
Libby quickly becomes friends with neighbor Angie, but there is something strange
about Angie's stepfather and when Libby learns the truth, she must make a very difficult
choice.
    ISBN 978-0-06-137597-2 (trade bdg.) — ISBN 978-0-06-137598-9 (lib. bdg.)
    [1. Friendship—Fiction. 2. Family problems—Fiction. 3. Stepfamilies—Fiction.
4. Moving, Household—Fiction. 5. Child sexual abuse—Fiction. 6. Racine (Wisc.)—
History—20th century—Fiction.] I. Title.
PZ7.C9093Whe 2008   2007018675
[Fic]—dc22   CIP
                                                                                                                            AC

Typography by Allison Limbacher
1 2 3 4 5 6 7 8 9 10
❖
First Edition

for Sean, my favorite

I'm made of rubber.

You're made of glue.

Everything you say bounces off me

and sticks on you.

Chapter 1

S he knocks on our door, but before anyone can answer it, she lets herself in. Our screen door opens, and a set of matching red toenails and fingernails appears as she moves her body through the door. She stands there expecting to be greeted like some kind of royalty.

Her eyes flash when she looks at me, as if I'd said something about her to someone and she had come over to knock me out.

I hope she isn't looking at anything in our living room. Our couch slumps in the middle, nothing matches, and the floors are a deep and dull brown from years of grime. Daddy made the end tables from wood he salvaged. Ma loves them and worries about their getting scratched every time we move.

I have on flip-flops and try not to act clumsy when I stand up even though the tips of my toes feel numb when I walk toward her. I don't know why, but right then and there I want her to like me.

Ma gives her a once-over before she says, "What's your name, young lady?" Young lady. That's Ma. Ma is normally nice, but if she doesn't take to you, you are dead, or nearly.

The girl looks at me as if to say, "Call off the dogs." She seems light-years older than I am, and I wonder if she's going to be a junior or senior and end up befriending Rita instead of me. "I'm Angie," she says. "Angie Bonar." Two beats later she adds, "Your house smells like lemons, ma'am."

Ma had been dusting with Lemon Pledge, a product made in this town.

"Well, pleased to meet you, Angie. I'm Mrs. Gilbert, and this is Libby. Libby Gilbert." Ma's tone is cold. I tell the girl we should go outside. I hold the screen door open for her.

When we get outside, Angie tells me we need to

vamos. She is taking me to the tracks.

"You've been here a week already." So she's been watching me. There is a pinched look to her that makes her face seem triangular and sharp. Her hair, long and light brown, is held back with a barrette at the top. Close up, Angie smells like soap and something salty. I tell her I'm not allowed. As soon as I say it, I want to take it back. I'll be going to high school this fall. I should be breaking the rules.

She says, "Nobody's allowed—so what?"

I don't look behind me or say anything to Ma. I slap my flip-flops down the crumbling sidewalk toward who knows what. As we walk the four blocks to the railroad tracks, I shrug off my mother's attitude. Isn't this what Daddy says moving is about? Opportunities. A chance to meet different people.

I ask Angie about how things work around here. She says Rubberville isn't a real place on the map; it's what people refer to when they mean our part of town; it's the nickname of a factory that was once here. There are boundaries in Rubberville: the tracks, the factories, the corner grocer, and the block near the sewer pipe shortcut. Lake Michigan is close, but not close enough. Angie's been living here as long as she can remember.

"As far back as the Phoenicians," she says.

"Who are they?"

"None of your business." Angie leaves it at that.

We pass the corner store, and Angie says a perfect pervert runs it; I need to be on the lookout when I go in. I look down when she says the word "pervert."

There's always someone in every neighborhood with loads of faith that it should be better, someone who puts out the reindeer or lucky elf statues, potted plants, and shiny pinwheels on sticks. That person in Rubberville is Mr. Ramirez, our neighbor, the one with the Foxy Lady van.

The day we moved in, Ma and Daddy argued about asking him to move it. The van has a beautiful Spanish lady's face painted on it. Sparkly letters in a script that looks puffy, like they were written with shaving cream, say "Foxy Lady." When I looked at it that first day, I got a sensation in my throat. Something about that face.

At the tracks I see thorny wild roses, bushes, rocks. Angie says the gravel is for throwing. Good for perfecting your aim. I pick up a little rock and watch it drop. Angie shows me the exact spot under the tracks where there's a sewer pipe big enough to walk through. That's the shortcut to take to school in the fall. She points into the distance at a brick building that looks almost like a castle. That is the parts factory.

"What grade *are* you anyway?" Angie asks.

I don't want to tell Angie I'm only going into ninth, that I'm not quite fifteen, but I tell her the truth. When she says, "Oh, yeah? Me too," I suddenly feel so much better, even though it's really hard to believe we're the same age.

Angie tells me that when people go to the bathroom on the train, it falls right out onto the tracks, number two and everything. I tell Angie there ought to be some law against that. She agrees. But in the meantime watch where you step. Keep your shoes on and you won't get lockjaw.

As we head down the embankment toward the sewer, she explains about her family. She's got an older brother, Frankie, a mother, and a stepdad. Kevin. I saw Kevin a week ago, the day we moved in. That day Angie was standing out in her front yard across the street from us. As she watched my family move in, Kevin walked up next to her and put his arm around her shoulder. He wore a leather vest without a shirt on and a pair of faded jeans. He had a headful of brown curly hair. He was barefoot. He squinted across the street at me to see what she was looking at. She looked up at him, just for a second, like she wanted to punch him in the stomach, like his touch on her shoulder was adding another five degrees to her temperature. That look stopped me from going over to her to say hello. Stopped me cold.

Usually when we move, me and Toby and Rita end up watching TV in a cruddy motel room somewhere on the edge of town, wishing there were at least a pool or a vending machine, while Ma and Daddy go looking for somewhere for us to live. Those are the times we get along best; we feel crazy and doomed together.

Our new town is Racine, in a state you can pronounce many ways. Wis-con-sin. You can say it fast or slow or emphasize the "w" or the "o" or even shorten it to "'sconsin." The city is located on Lake Michigan between Milwaukee and Chicago. When I first took a look around our neighborhood and saw the overcast houses, I couldn't imagine there'd be someplace worse. The houses are small, the paint on them fading from weather and neglect. Short fences, some picket, some chain-link, ring the perimeter of each bare yard, making the houses seem even smaller. The idea of having to live in one made my heart slow to nothing.

And the factories in the area are noisy and smell like engine grease up close. Ma said Milwaukee has tanneries and breweries. "Think about that," she said.

Our neighborhood is located on what used to be cabbage fields for Frank's Sauerkraut before the factories came. All the houses used to be for migrant workers. They've all had rooms added on over time. The rooms are cramped, and the floors tilt every which way, like a fun house without the fun. Trains cut through what used to be the fields to go to the factories. I can't tell if it's cabbage or rubber or garbage I'm smelling when I go outside.

When we first walked into the house, Ma said, "Whew," and then, "Oh, boy," and "We've got a lot of cleaning up to do."

But then my sister, Rita, let loose. She'd been keeping quiet and keeping score. Rita said she couldn't believe we'd moved into this dinky pigsty, with some ridiculous disco van parked out front. Both of Rita's hands were on her hips; her dark hair, messed up from moving, hung in greasy hanks around her face. Normally she's very pretty, her hair done perfectly in a flippy shag.

But that day she was beside herself. Her shorts were dirty, and her makeup was smudged. She said she was done being a good sport; she was too old to start with new friends. She'd be a junior in a high school where everyone already had friends. "Libby's going to be a freshman," she said, "and that's not as bad." Her anger filled up the entire kitchen, and there was nowhere for it to go.

Ma pushed her brown hair, laced with strands of gray, back behind her ears, pulled a few bobby pins out of her pocket, and pinned her hair in place while she looked out the window at the street. I stepped up behind her to see what she was looking at. Her eyes were fixed on the van. The woman's face painted on the van beamed out at us like those sad child clown pictures. Behind her brown, wild hair, rays of light haloed the back of her Foxy Lady head. I believed she knew how it felt to be in a family like mine. Daddy said, "The van is staying put, and so are we." Ma's shoulders sagged. Rita fumed. My brother, on the other hand, looked gorgeous and dangerous, like his idol, Bruce Springsteen. His long dark bangs hung over one eye; he had his hands in his pockets. I couldn't tell if he was trying to hide them or control them.

On the wall, the last renter had kept a calendar, marking off each day with an X as if every day done had been one day closer to being released from prison. The photo on the calendar was a bottle of something called Crown Royal, and it was peeling off under the headline "Compliments of Arbee's Liquor Store." The last day X'd was two days ago, June 15, the same day we left Mississippi.

I follow Angie to the sewer pipe. It smells musty at the opening.

"Hey, I dare you to walk through."

"There's no way I'm walking through that thing," I say. What a bad shortcut, I think, even though I can see to the other side just fine.

"Libby. Honestly." Angie, disappointed, puts her hands on her hips.

I hold my breath and go.

Afterward she says, "Here, brave girl. Have a Now-and-Later. Watermelon."

"I love these." I'm doubly glad she didn't offer me a cigarette.

I take the wax-wrapped square from her hand. It is warm. The unwrapped candy sticks to my teeth. I suck hard on it, bite down. Angie flips hers around in her mouth.

We walk the tracks together. I don't quite have the hang of it. It's a lot like staying on the balance beam, and I'm no good at that. Angie demonstrates how to stay on. You don't grip your toes too hard, and you keep your knees bent. Arms go out to the side like a ballerina's, but not over your head—unless you want to show off. When both our arms are out ballerina style, we touch our fingertips together. Then her hand rests on my arm, while mine grips hers too tight, but she doesn't stop me. I feel my fingernails dig into her flesh. I look at the marks my fingernails put in her arm. I hold on.

We hear rumbling.

I smell the oily gravel, some dead animal, maybe in the bushes. I head straight into them as the noise gets louder. The branches scratch my bare arms.

"C'mon, Libby." Angie reaches back for me when I see the train. It is coming fast down the tracks. I crouch down. We have to get out of the way.

"C'mon, Libby, I dare you."

"No." I tell her I have to go.

"Don't, please," she says.

"Okay, I won't." I hope I don't regret it.

Angie crouches down to sit by me near the bushes but then starts clawing at my shirt. I see the train's engine in full view. Her hands scratch my chest through my shirt as she grasps a handful of fabric and yanks. As she pulls me up, she grabs me from behind and pushes me toward the oncoming train. She holds my arms tight behind my back. I struggle to get away.

We are right up to the tracks, just a couple of feet away, when we hear the engineer's warning whistle blast in our ears. I try stomping on her feet, but she grips me tighter and knees the back of my legs. Then I feel the airstream of the train batter our bodies.

I stop struggling when I see how the car wheels stay on the tracks, the pistons rotating faster than the individual wheels as the passenger train goes past. It is the miracle of gravity. The cars sway to this side and that. Close up it seems like the cars tip too far over. The train goes fast, each light between the cars a moment's hesitation, rhythmic and even. The momentum from it goes right under my skin, pulsing with a force that feels good. It surges through me, and I am taken over. I can't hear anything but a tunneling sound; I taste the oily dust.

That surge inside my body breaks down and goes away as I watch the caboose get smaller and smaller. Angie lets me go.

"Did you see that?" I ask, breaking the spell.

"Yeah, every day, just about."

"Does your mom know?"

"Yeah." Angie shrugs. No big deal.

"And she doesn't stop you?"

We both look down the tracks. The train is gone. The sky is blue-blue, and the clouds are collecting in cottony puffs. Nothing moved; nothing to worry about. We are in a dream, not a particularly good one, I realize, but at least we're in it together.

Chapter 2

I look at the little silvery alewives, stiff and dried up, lining the whole shoreline. They are tangled in one another's bones, and they smell. Hundreds of staring fish eyes are pointed at us.

We bring blankets to lie on at the beach and towels to share among the five of us. Rita is hogging one whole blanket and a towel for herself. Her white-ass body is in a bikini. Ma and Rita fought about that. Guess who won. Daddy swings around toward me and Rita and declares today's a day to relax, cool off after our big move. At the beach house, boys stand around on the terrace, watching. Rita doesn't have the nerve or the suntan to go up there yet, but it's only a matter of time.

The beach house is an old sandstone building with a snack bar and bathrooms. It looks like a fortress, solid against the wind. Flimsy fences surround it. North Beach itself is at least a mile long, and the beach house, near the parking lot, is quite a distance from the shore of Lake Michigan. Everyone has plenty of space to spread out.

The sand is burning hot. Toby goes to the beach house to get us some popcorn, and he looks as if he's walking on hot coals to get there; his knees rise and fall in an awkward rhythm. I smile, knowing my brother is still willing to cross hot sand for us. He is really biding his time before he leaves us for good, because this is his senior year. Ever since he discovered Bruce Springsteen, he's spent less time being a nice big brother and more time listening to the same CDs over and over in his bedroom. The howling sounds that come out of the CD player seem to push him to get mad at things for no reason that I can see. I guess those songs just got into him. Something's happening inside him, a concoction in the soul, one part brother to two parts Springsteen.

Ma shifts her body to the center of the other blanket. Her swimsuit is a polka-dot one-piece. She still has a good figure. The wind blows her hair into her eyes.

I notice a little hole in the side of Ma's suit I'd not seen before. I poke it with my fingernail, and she slaps my hand, hard, and says, "Libby, knock it off." I tell her to make Rita share.

"Rita can have that blanket," Ma says, putting a shoe on each corner of the blanket she's been sitting on, to keep it from blowing up in the breeze. Ma must be trying some kind of reverse psychology, letting Rita know how selfish she is by giving her what she wants.

I go stand with Daddy at the edge of the water. He lights up a cigarette. I press close to him, taste cigarette smoke as he exhales through his nose. He looks royal to me, thin dark hair, a hint of stubbornness at the mouth, as if he's about to command a great army. His veins are definitely blue. Daddy doesn't want Ma or Rita to be mad about the move. He's taking us to the Dairy Queen later. It's part of the cycle. We move; we get a treat; Daddy hates his job; we move again. Daddy will start work tomorrow. We all are trying not to get our hopes up.

The lake water seeps under the soles of my feet. I ask Daddy if the lake water came from the North Pole, from some melted glacier. He nods and says, "Uh-huh, that's why this is one of the Great Lakes." He tells me how to remember them all: HOMES. Huron, Ontario, Michigan, Erie, Superior. Our lake, Lake Michigan, is one of the biggest. The feeling that an ice cube is slowly melting underfoot gradually sneaks up my legs, but my heart stops cold when Daddy says, "I think this lake is our lucky charm, Libby." Optimism is always part of the new beginning.

He puts out his cigarette in the sand and pockets the stub in his swim trunks.

Daddy says, "There's a sandbar out a little ways. Walk out there with me."

I tell him, "I will if you don't try to make me swim." There is no way in hell I'm swimming.

He says okay. He always insists that I should learn how to swim, but every time I get in the water and have to put my face down into it, I can't do it. It's the idea of all that water getting into my nose and filling up my ears. I know that's what it must be like to be inside a seashell, everything sounding far away, water clogging the shell's inner chamber. Underwater, all I feel is strangulation rising in my throat. I come up coughing each and every time, Daddy patting my back, saying, "Libby, this is ridiculous. You have to learn to swim; you just have to."

Instead of getting me to try it today, he just says, "We'll get to know this lake little by little." We get into the water to our thighs, and I go numb to my feet but keep walking. Suddenly we're in ankle-deep water again. Daddy says that boats have to be careful of sandbars so they don't get stuck or grounded. I keep waiting for him to push me, the way Angie pushed me toward the train, to try to get me to swim, but he doesn't. Still, I move a little farther from him.

A breeze is coming from the direction of the snack bar, carrying the smell of cotton candy and popcorn. I look for Toby but don't see him. From where we're standing, Ma and Rita look like the pictures of sea monkeys you see in comic books. Me and Daddy wave at them and then walk back through the icy water to the shore. The sun is hot on my shoulders. Its warmth keeps my teeth from chattering. The brightness of the sun reflected on the water reassembles something inside my chest.

The lake's waves are wide and lazy, and other kids play in the water as if the water were coming from a faucet. When we get back to shore, Daddy crouches at the edge. He looks childlike, especially in those blue swim trunks. Summer after summer he wears the same swim trunks. At least there are some things about my daddy that are reliable.

ME AND TOBY have been making sand castles, one after the other, some kind of castle assembly line.

"It's a way to start things over," he says.

I wonder if we should be making sand castles anymore, bent over in the sand like little kids, but if he still wants to do it, I guess it's okay.

I've been making my castles with flat roofs and jagged tops, letting the sand flow between my fingers. Toby's fingers are playing with the wet sand, making a mound that looks like a giant teardrop. He keeps on making mounds, joining them with stick bridges. He said that the castles from long ago were pretty much nothing to look at, just a way to keep the enemy from sneaking up on you.

I wonder what's dogging my brother. His chest is

covered with curly black hairs, and underneath it all is something still and serious. It's hard to make bridges out of twigs and driftwood. The bridge he's working on collapses into the moat again.

After a couple of hours in the sun, my face feels tight and windburned. I look at all we've done. We've got moats galore, castle towers filled to the brim, some with warriors and others with princesses, sticks with gum wrappers stuck on the tops, seagull feathers posted at the entrance to the kingdom, and a sandy wall guarding it all. Toby even dug a lake that fills up from the waves coming and going on the shore. A little silvery fish, a live one, got trapped in it. We looked at it awhile, the shiny fish flipping about, causing little sand clouds in the water. I wanted to keep it, take it home. Toby picked up the fish and threw it back into the lake. We'd invented a whole new world, but we couldn't really expect anything to live in it. Our sand castles turn whiter and rounder in the sun's glare before Daddy tells us it's time to go.

ACROSS THE STREET from the Dairy Queen is a building that looks like a flying saucer. It's called the Golden Rondelle, and it's a movie theater for nature shows that's in the shape of a gold oval bubble.

"What kind of crazy guy made that?" Toby asks. We both really like it, even though it makes no sense as a building and is surrounded by a floor-wax company parking lot.

Daddy says the Golden Rondelle came from outer space to deliver an important message to earthlings about the future, and the message got ignored.

We pull into the Dairy Queen parking lot, and Daddy and Rita refuse to get out of the car. Daddy won't because he never does, and Rita won't because she said she doesn't want to look like some little kid standing in line. So me, Ma, and Toby make our way toward the service window. We are the only whites. We are also the only people who are related to a Bruce Springsteen look-alike. Nobody here seems to care about either. A nasal girl, a hairnet plastered to her forehead, greets us.

Daddy likes nuts, so he gets a cone with peanuts on top; Rita and Ma get sundaes; me and Toby go for Dilly Bars. Ma pays for all of it with a worn-out twenty-dollar bill Daddy gave her. Money can look old anytime, I know, but this bill seems to be the last one he earned before we moved here. Although I eat my Dilly Bar in tiny licks, it falls apart right at the end, right before I get down to the stick. The chocolate coating crumbles on me.

"Jesus, Libby. You dropped chocolate all over." Rita wants to know why I always have to make a big mess.

"Why should you care? It's not on you." I pick up the pieces melting on my thigh and put them in my mouth.

"What a baby," Rita says, and turns her head away in disgust.

Ma looks away, eats her sundae slowly, as if she has all week to finish it. Toby wolfed his bar in two seconds flat with no time to melt, same as Daddy.

Toby's been watching the teenagers by the garbage cans play with one another, shoving, swearing, and laughing. He looks at them as if he should know them from somewhere.

"Can we go home?"

THE HOUSE IS still hot when we get home, and the cool from the lake and the ice cream has worn off. Since tomorrow is Daddy's first day at his new job, he says he's going to polish his shoes. I ask if I can help, and he says sure, but mostly I just watch from a seat at the kitchen table.

The shoeshine box is pretty fancy. Daddy made it himself. The box has two side doors that lift up, one side for storing the dark polishes, the other for keeping the white polish. "A good side and a bad side," Daddy joked when he showed me how he set up the box with the color logic in mind.

On top of the box is a platform about the width of a man's shoe and a foot long. Daddy put a strip of ribbed rubber on it to keep shoes from slipping as they were getting shined. He said you can tell a lot about a person by the state of his shoes. He opens the dark polish side of the box. Black marks riddle the wood inside.

There's a pile of stained flannel rags in the box. He says Ma's old nighties are the best for a shine. He smiles at her. "Your mother's got more than a few of those granny gowns to spare."

"Do you have to do that in here, Wayne?" Ma says. "I won't be able to put the food on the table until you're done."

Ma waves her hand at the air, swatting an invisible bug. I can see the bra straps she's forever pushing up under the sleeves. She looks out the window behind her before turning back to the stove. The sun is nearly set. If I look too hard in that direction, my eyes water.

Daddy turns his attention back to me, forcing Ma to wait. "Polishing your shoes is like having an oil change for the car," he says. "You get a lot more wear and tear out of them for just a little bit of work." I wonder if any of the men Daddy will work with go to the trouble.

Daddy puts one worn shoe on his left hand and rubs in the black polish with the other. Then he does the other shoe. "They have to dry a sec," he says. The weirdly plastic smell of the polish overrides the smell of hamburger in the kitchen.

Daddy palms a stiff brush and begins brushing the shoes, holding them up to the light. I'm not sure what he's looking for. Then he puts them on his feet and sets one foot up on the shoeshine platform. His back is curved, lumpy with muscle and bone. His shoulders shimmy back and forth as he pulls the soft cloth over each shoe. He puts everything he has into the movements: his irritation with Ma; our worries about money; his eagerness to make a good first impression. All I can see is his back, but I know his forehead is furrowed with thought lines. When he stops, the shoes are shining, almost like new.

Chapter 3

When I get to Angie's back door, she tilts her head away from the screen toward what's inside and practically threatens me. "We are going straight to my room, Libby. No stopping. No staring."

I step inside behind Angie and hear music playing. When we walk into the kitchen, the woman listening to it turns around.

It's too late. I am already staring.

A round and very made-up mouth says to Angie, "Now who do we have here?" Angie mumbles something that sounds like Middy Delbert.

"Pleased to meet you, Mrs. Bonar," I say. I can't

take my eyes off her, and I can't think of anything else to say. This is like those phone calls with Grandma. After she asks about my grades, there's nothing left to talk about.

"You just call me Char, honey," she says. "Oh. I'm also not a Bonar, just that girl and her brother." Mrs. Not-Bonar nods toward Angie, her shadowed eyes looking through locks of streaked and teased hair. Angie told me her stepdad has a thing about hair. He said guys like hair they can bury their face in, hair without a lot of shit in it.

The house looks like some bomb went off in it, exploding clothes and towels and sports equipment. There are things draped over every chair, and the couch is crowded with coats and purses. The living room windows are covered with an opaque gold fabric that keeps the house clammy and dim. Some of the pins that hold the drapes in place have fallen out, and the pleats fan out under the rod.

Angie's brother is in his room listening to music with headphones on. He's singing along. His legs are crossed, and a sweat sock is dangling off his left foot. Crap is strewn all over the floor of his room: shoes and clothes and records. Nearly every square inch of wall space is covered with posters of cars and rock stars.

He doesn't see us pass.

Angie says, "My brother, Frankie. He disgusts me," and lifts her chin as we pass by. I can't help turning my head and keep looking; the jangle of guitars from the headphones sounds tinny and far away.

Angie's room looks like it does not even belong in her house. It is so sunny and neat. Angie's curtains have a pink flower print that matches the bedspread that matches the pillow shams, and the bed frame matches the dresser and desk. It's all one whole set. Angie even has her own stereo. She's got what looks like the Swiss Alps mountains, horses, and dogs painted on cardboard and propped up on the dresser's edge by the mirror. Getting to Angie's room is like letting out a held breath. It is the perfect hangout.

Angie says, "Libby, always, always, always close the door behind you."

We both plop on her bed. She asks why I haven't been able to see her the last couple of days. I tell her I went with Ma to clean houses, that I did it because I want to make some money this summer. I don't want her to think I always have to listen to my mother. Angie looks at me hard. She knows I'm full of it.

Angie says she has something to show me, but I can't stop looking around her room. My room doesn't have any pictures or posters. Me and Rita have matching green bedspreads, but no flower anything, no pretty rugs. She tells me nearly everything in her room is from Kevin, her stepdad. "I can always get him to buy me things," she says.

"How do you do that?" I ask. I tell her about how I begged and begged my daddy for a pony before I finally gave up. I was getting nowhere.

"He just does," she answers. "I can't explain it."

A zebra-striped rug is thrown over the top of the rag rug on the floor by her bed. I ask her how come her room is so nice and neat, and she says that's the way she wants it. She doesn't want to sleep in a pigsty, even if the rest of the house has gone to hell.

Angie gets up and opens her closet, and I see rows of clothes arranged by type and color. Angie pushes aside some things in her closet. She pulls out a picture of a brown horse and foal. It looks as if she painted it with one of those sets. The mare has a white stripe down the center of her forehead. The foal is long-legged but looks just like the mother, white stripe and light brown haunches. The mane and tail on both are black. They are standing by a split rail fence. "Wait," she says. She hands me the painting and goes back into her closet. She pulls out another one exactly like it, but this time the horses are more tan than brown and have white manes and tails. Palominos.

"Which one do you want?"

I look them both over. "So you're going to give me one to take home?" I have to check to make sure, because maybe it could be mine, but only when I come over. She nods.

I like the one with the palominos. That's the one I want.

"I knew it," she says. "I want that one too."

I take the other one, just to be nice. It's second best, but nobody has ever thought enough to make a painting for me, especially of my favorite subject, horses. It's a nice thing to do. It's things like that Ma wouldn't understand about Angie.

"Libby, you know what? At the end of July are pony rides at the Elmwood Plaza sidewalk sale. Last year I helped with the ponies. Maybe this year you can too."

My head nearly floats off my shoulders, as I think about the possibility.

The sound of movement from the other side of the bedroom door causes me to stand abruptly and let out a breath I didn't know I was holding. Angie reaches for the doorknob. Her brother, Frankie, opens the door without knocking.

Angie's face changes. "What do *you* want?"

Frankie looks me over. He's another version of Angie, light eyes and a triangle face, but taller, with light hair to his shoulders and a necklace, a macramé and shell creation.

"Kevin's home. He wants to see you. Downstairs."

My heart is beating a little faster than it should.

"Hey, who's that?" Frankie points rudely at me. "What grade are you in?"

"None of your beeswax." Angie's eyes are locked on her brother. "Tell Kevin I've got company."

Angie slams the door on him. "Asshole." The sound goes straight into my shoulder blades.

"Kevin wants me to practice pool with him. He

said I could be a female Minnesota Fats. It's the dumbest thing." Angie says it's the dumbest thing, but she sounds glad about it. She sits down on the bed.

"Your brother seems like a jerk."

"Libby, why don't you just sit down?"

I flop down on Angie's bed again and wonder if I should go home. Ma warned me that making friends too fast is making friends with Trouble.

I remember the last friend I had. A girl named Doris who was very clean and pale and perfect. She taught me how to crochet granny squares and do macramé. When I went to her house, time crawled to a stop even though we usually had a snack and milk. An hour there felt like five. We were friends because she wanted another merit badge for Girl Scouts. Before I left, she showed it to me, already sewed to the sash that decorated the drab green dress she loved to wear on meeting day. Each one of those colorful patches meant some good deed. Doris pointed to the one she earned on my account, a little yellow teacup embroidered onto a green circle. A hospitality award.

My new friend pulls out CDs and records I've never heard of. She can't believe I've never heard of the singers and bands she listens to. I can't believe she's never heard of Bruce Springsteen.

"Libby, where did you come from? Some kind of hick town?" That's exactly how I feel hanging out with her.

She looks at me with pity, hands on her hips.

"I was going through my mom's old records when I found this one. I can't stop listening to it."

"Shut up, Angie. Just play your dumb record, okay?"

She turns her back on me as she pulls a Peter Frampton record out of its sleeve.

She tells me to just stay down on the bed. "Once you hear it, you will be in heaven."

Angie starts to sing when the music comes on: "'I'm in yoooo, you're in meeee—' what do you think, Libby? Pretty good, huh?" She kisses Frampton's face on the record cover.

He is pretty good, this guy. His voice is smooth, not at all like the records my brother likes. His song has a way of making me feel things really could be better in Rubberville. Angie tosses Peter to the floor and bounces onto the bed next to me, puts her head on a pillow, hands over her head. "I could listen to him all day."

She turns toward me. "I wish you were my sister."

I think about what that would be like, a sister who wouldn't say, "Don't touch anything of mine or I'll kill you," and wouldn't be so sulky, like Rita. Someone like Angie, who wants to hang out with me.

Angie's wearing the same shirt from the day she took me to the tracks; it has little roses cascading down and around the front and ties at the neck and elbows. I tell her it's nice.

"Nice, huh? Would you like it? Let's trade."

"You want my shirt? This T-shirt?" I paw the purple T-shirt I'm wearing.

"Sure." Then she says, "Hey, dummy, you got to take your shirt *off* to trade."

I swallow. She's serious. I take a deep breath and pull my T-shirt over my head. I have nothing on underneath. Angie sucks in her breath. I cross my arms over my chest, embarrassed. I look at her.

"Nothing." She shrugs and starts to take off her top. As she lifts her chin to pull it over her head, I see a reddish purple scuff within the smooth pale skin under her jawbone. Then I can't stop looking at her bra as Angie helps me into the shirt she wants me to try on. I feel her fingers on my torso as she helps me pull the shirt down, smoothing out wrinkles. "Stand still. Hold out your arms." We are this close. I can't forget I am totally naked under her shirt.

Angie reaches behind my neck and pulls a few hairs out of the collar. "You look good," she says.

She fluffs up my hair a little and then puts on my T-shirt. She rolls into me on the bed with her face on my chest. Her hair falls over my left arm. It tickles, and I laugh. There's a knock on the door. Angie says, "I am not getting up off this bed. Tell Frankie fuck-face we're busy," she whispers.

"Hey, uh, we don't want to see you," I yell to Frankie. "You can't come in. It's locked." Me and Angie laugh into her matching pillow shams. An electric sensation spreads through my middle. It feels good to lie.

Angie laughs out loud but then gets up and goes to the door. She smiles at me before she opens it. I suddenly feel betrayed. Kevin looks surprised to see me, and that makes two of us.

UP CLOSE KEVIN'S almost as pretty as the Foxy Lady. He has brown curly hair, with brown eyes to match and perfectly straight teeth. I notice the teeth because when he smiles at us, they are just gorgeous. Looking at him, I turn to rubber.

The rec room is in the basement. There's a collection of beer cans taking up almost an entire wall, showcasing scenes of nature and football teams. The area stinks like baby powder. I guess everyone puts it on the pool cues and it's everywhere. But I love the picture of a sock with a toe sticking out. It says, "A Hole in One."

"Ladies," he says. Very sweet. He nods toward me. Someone must have taught him manners. Unlike Frankie.

I feel stupid wearing Angie's shirt now and wonder if he recognizes it.

"Frankie said you want me to go to hell." Kevin looks amused and not at all mad. He looks clean and freshly showered as he decides on a pool cue.

I wonder if he works at the parts factory too, if he's met Daddy.

Angie pushes her right hip out toward Kevin when he turns around. She leans on the pool table and crosses her arms. She tosses her hair and stares straight into his eyes. Neither says anything more, as if they've just made a bet: The one who talks first is the loser.

Finally, Angie smiles up at Kevin and says, "Frankie's a big fat liar," and turns back toward me and says, "Isn't he?"

I don't say anything. I feel jealousy pulse through my arms. I close my eyes for a minute—anything to erase Angie's faced tipped toward Kevin's. He leans his face in close to hers. I wonder what she feels like inside my clothes. "Your mother wouldn't believe you either. Don't make me have to tell your mother what a sassy young lady she's raising," he whispers loud enough for me to hear. He turns around to grab a pool cue, and I see his muscles are tense in his shirt.

Angie starts putting pool balls into this triangle on top of the pool table. She tells me that this is called racking and that the solid balls have to alternate with the stripy ones. The black eight ball has to be in the middle of the triangle. Both Kevin and I watch her rack. Kevin absently puts blue chalk on the tip of his pool cue while waiting for her to finish.

When Angie's done, Kevin puts the chalk down. "Generally, when you rack, the yellow number one ball goes at the head of the triangle and the eight ball takes center position in the third row, which is the closest thing to the middle of the triangle," he says.

Once Angie sets everything in its place, she carefully lifts the triangle off the arrangement. When she gets ready to break, as she says, Kevin steps in. As she bends over the pool table with a pool cue, he comes from behind and leans over her. Taking her cue in his hands, he tells her to relax her left index finger and grip the cue more firmly in her right hand.

"Like this." He demonstrates and puts his hand over hers. Angie turns and looks up at Kevin, then down at the pool table as if she can't decide.

I curl my fingers into fists. I take a deep breath and inhale the baby powder and the smell of stale beer from behind the bar to the right of the pool table. I think about the crusty pan with baked noodles I saw in the kitchen sink, the messy counter. I listen to the hum of the refrigerator in the corner of the basement.

"Then give the cue ball a jab, like this." His right arm tenses over hers, and Angie's right arm follows. The balls break apart in one big clack that seems to smack the inside of my head.

Chapter 4

Our kitchen seems even smaller when four of Daddy's new buddies from work pack down on our rickety wooden chairs to talk shop. It's hard to say they're really buddies like me and Angie, but they are trying hard to be friendly with one another even if they seem to be disagreeing about everything. They lift their cans of beer and cigarettes toward the light hanging from the ceiling when they make a point. The men in the kitchen seem so strong compared with Daddy, who is wiry more than anything. Their muscles flex when they move even an inch. Everyone but Daddy is wearing a gray work shirt with his name embroidered above the words "Parts Division." Every single one of them can fix anything that has a motor.

Ma and Rita are helping Daddy by serving coffee, beers, and snacks out of bags. I'm sure the pervert from the corner store was happy to finally have a sale over two dollars from us. I'm sitting in the doorway, but Toby's got a seat at the table, listening to the men in the kitchen. This meeting is important to Daddy, but Ma got home late, and our place doesn't look very good. There are greasy fingerprints on the wall by the phone and crumbs on the floor. Dishes are stacked in the sink, with leftovers hardened on them. I know she's embarrassed, but I bet their houses look just as bad.

All the men have the same routine as Daddy when they get home. Metal shavings from the parts and engines end up on the floor of the shop. They call them chips, and they get stuck in the bottoms of everyone's shoes. Daddy pulls them out one by one with a tweezers or sometimes a flathead screwdriver, and he talks about his day. He jokes that the chips should be worth money, like at a casino. If he pulls out more than ten chips per shoe, he'll also pull a

Hershey's chocolate bar out of his pocket to prove there is still generosity in the world.

Daddy really wants to be his own boss, so every time he gets a job, it's like he's already failed. He see-saws between taking regular jobs and creating businesses that never get off the ground.

We've ended up in Rubberville because Daddy's last moneymaking scheme didn't work out.

Nightcrawlers. "You don't have to do hardly nothing, and they'll reproduce, they're *hermaphroditic*, you know," said the man who set Daddy up. I found out that meant the worms were boy and girl in one.

Daddy laid out the money for the worms and the buckets they lived in even though Ma was against it.

We had a sign on the road in an area known as a sportsman's paradise. NIGHTCRAWLERS FOR SALE. There were nightcrawler businesses all over Mississippi, we came to find out, people with the same idea—that you could make a pile of money doing nothing. Not too many people stopped to buy our worms. When they did, we would scoop them out into a special container we supplied the customer. The worm salesman said you couldn't just up and use a coffee can. What you catch when you go fishing depends on the mood and quality of the worms. "These worms are special," he said through his nostrils. "People won't know that if you put them in any old thing." Daddy agreed.

Daddy kept his job at the other farm and left us to take care of the worm business. When Ma used a scoop to get at the worms, she'd accidentally chop them in half, all to keep the dirt out from under her nails. Rita refused to touch them, but me and Toby grabbed them in clumps with our bare hands. We liked to feel the blind squirm of them.

Somehow all the worms suffocated and died. There we were with buckets of starved and shriveled worms. Nothing could be done to save them. In the end Daddy sold the whole lot of them for next to nothing to someone who wanted them for compost. Ma said, "Black gold to him, dead dirt to us." The special containers for customers got left behind. There was nothing else to do with them.

Now Daddy makes parts for engines. Ma's cleaning houses, something that gets her fingernails even dirtier.

Daddy says we live in the land of opportunity—a man can do whatever he wants in this country, and he just needs to work hard and have a little luck, that's all. I guess it's the little luck that's been missing so far. Every chip Daddy pulls out of the bottom of his shoes is a small piece broken away from some bigger dream.

Everyone at the table says thanks real polite when Rita fetches another beer or pours another cup of coffee or empties the ashtray or opens another bag of something. Rita has a way of turning her body at certain angles and pulling her bangs back so they fall in a lazy sweep over one eye. Every time she does something, one or another of the men is acting as if he'd like to jump up and help her out with it, like how Kevin teaches Angie to play pool. That's exactly what Rita wants, men to fall all over her, but I'm surprised she's willing to act like a maid to get that kind of attention.

At the sink Ma tells Rita she's done enough and can go. Rita tells Ma all she wants to do is help. Ma's features go hard. She doesn't say more. Rita tosses her dish towel toward the counter and leaves the kitchen. "It's not fair," she whispers to me as she passes through the doorway to the living room.

Ma's wearing these goofy elastic pants with the

seam running down the legs and some checkered shirt. Even so, she's thin enough and shapely under there. But her movements are nothing like Rita's; she is in continual motion, moving through a screen of cigarette smoke that makes her look far away.

Toby notices me and nods slightly, as if we are both spies who will report to our army later. He's sitting between Daddy and a guy named Carl. Daddy said Toby could stay at the table because he's almost a man now.

Toby's just been hired at an auto body shop this summer. King of Kars, where Toby works, is located on a side street next to a motorcycle shop and a missionary church. Dave Dolan owns the shop. For Dave and Toby, cars are more than vehicles; they are a source of inspiration. They say they practice the art of auto body repair.

"What car you driving?" is a Rubberville greeting. My brother says what you're driving can tell a person everything about you in the same way Daddy says you can tell about someone by his shoes. Driving a dreaded import? You think you're so smart. A mini-van? You're getting by. A Caddie with no rust? You are seriously in debt. A station wagon like ours?

You're trying to get out of debt. A Jaguar? You're from Chicago, you're a drug dealer, and you're screwing someone over. The Foxy Lady van—that's just crazy.

Dave claims he's giving my brother a shot at a decent living and Toby is fucking it up. He told my brother a guy should be out getting pussy, not going around pretending he's Springsteen. He says that's just like going around telling everyone you're a big fat faggot.

Toby puts up with it because he wants money to buy a car. As for me, I want horsepower of a different kind. My own real horse.

The men laugh a little bit when Daddy says, "The union says we gotta give management time to respond." Management. It's a dirty word. The men say the foreman is a problem. They can't wait on the union. They don't like his attitude. He prowls the aisles saying things about how stupid one guy is or how they got rid of a guy for just that, so watch it.

Ma has heard enough talk about what to do about uppity foremen. She's just so tired of it. Daddy says fairness isn't a part of the system. Not just fairness at work, but the bigger kind of fairness. The kind where any guy can make a living and keep a family together without worrying about what's next, feeling like there's no say in what happens just because you need a job so damn bad. Then my brother says Bruce Springsteen sings about men with just those kinds of problems. Everyone looks at my brother and then at Ma and Daddy. Ma and Daddy just look down at their hands.

One of the men at the table says the foreman used to be a regular guy before he got promoted, that now he's part of the problem but not all of it. He's worried all machines will be put together by robots in the future and the only ones left with jobs will be the robots. "All these years of learning to do motors just to get your job ripped right out from under you by a robot." I wish housecleaning jobs would go to robots.

On my first housecleaning outing Ma told me to clean Mrs. Rutger's house as if it were my own. Otherwise the leftover dirt would bother her conscience. Never mind that we don't actually clean our own house because Ma's too busy working.

Carl gestures with his head toward next door. "That wetback's willing to work for next to nothing just to put gas in the disco van." His crack about

Mr. Ramirez makes my ears go hot. Everyone but Daddy laughs.

Toby looks torn; he wants to laugh but knows he shouldn't. Daddy says, "What the hell does any van have do with anything? There are certain reasons people do things," Daddy says, "and it's a tough world out there, but sometimes the reasons to do something can be real personal, something besides getting a dollar more an hour."

I silently agree with Daddy. Mr. Ramirez certainly has good reasons for putting the picture of the Foxy Lady on his van. He has something he wants to tell the world. In order for anyone to notice, he needs to put her face out there. But why a lady instead of a sunset or something like that?

The sound of a TV show about a black kid in New York who goes to an all-white school wafts in from the living room, the canned laughter coming at all the wrong times for the talk going on in the kitchen. Rita's been sulking on the couch, watching. Her face looks blue in the light from the TV screen.

Instead of watching, I grab a stack of home decorating magazines Mrs. Rutger gave Ma and look busy. Mrs. Rutger turned out to be okay. She keeps giving things to Ma. She thinks she's helping us out.

I sit with my back against the kitchen wall while the men talk, browsing through one of the magazines. Bright rugs in psychedelic colors swirl through nothing but white, white, white. White walls, white couches, white appliances.

I look at a gleaming swimming pool featured in the magazine and wonder what it would be like filled with milk. More white. The lady of the house collects art in her spare time, jetting the world to find sculptures that she thinks go well in her light box of a house.

I look at the macramé owl I made last year hanging on the paneled wall in our kitchen. The knots are orderly and flat, comforting. So are Angie's paint-by-numbers paintings.

I ended up taking the second-best brown horse with the black mane the day she asked me to pick, even though I tried to talk myself into taking the other one. I love it more now, because after I decided, Angie said she'd fix it. She painted flames around the horses in the paddock and signed her name in a heart at the bottom. That was her first step to being a real artist, she said.

Ma helped me hang Angie's horse painting on the wall in my bedroom, even after Rita protested. Rita makes sure to tell me how ugly she thinks it is about ten times a day.

She said, "Do we have to look at stupid shit everywhere we turn? First it's that stupid van, now this stupid horse and fire thing." Rita believes that the stupidity of Rubberville should be overcome, but in my opinion she's picking the wrong things to focus on. To me, Angie's picture is about horses overcoming their greatest fear, fire. I've looked at it so much, I understand that the picture was incomplete before the flames were added.

Ma surprised me by sticking up for it and told Rita she's just jealous nobody has ever painted a picture for her.

The air is thick with fed-up voices. Carl says they need to find out if the union will get behind them. They need to have a plan of action. Daddy says Carl's right; they shouldn't just jump into it. They need to be strategic.

A guy named Harvey says his biggest consideration is his family, how they're going to make it. Harvey hasn't said much until now. He seems to be the type to listen to everyone say their piece before letting anyone know what he thinks. When he talks, he looks at the dirt under his fingernails, as if he's talking to his hands instead of to the other men. "And scabs. That's something to consider too," Harvey says. Everyone nods.

It seems they'll all be out of jobs soon no matter what. I want to leave Rubberville, but not that way. Not again. Now that I have Angie as a friend, I feel differently about things.

AFTER THEY LEAVE, Ma and Daddy have it out.

"Wayne, I can't believe you want to get involved this way," Ma says.

"*No guts, no glory,* Martha," says Daddy. Even though I'm lying in bed in the dark, I can see the naughty grin on Daddy's face. I wish I could wipe it off, make him think about what he's doing to all of us.

"Honestly. Be serious." Ma's trying to humor him.

The air around me acts like a bad temper, hot and mean. The kitchen light is still on, and its light makes its way into the bedroom from under the door. I close my eyes against it.

"Rita? Are you still awake?" I ask the bunk below mine.

"Yeah." She doesn't sound a speck sleepy.

"Are you worried about what's going on?"

"No," she says. I know she's lying. It is so hard to talk to Rita lately. She thinks nobody understands her, what she's going through, having to move all the time. Now that I have Angie, I don't need her the way I used to. I think that upsets her too. She liked to know that she was everything to me.

I can tell Daddy is smoking. There's a quiet between him and Ma that goes on too long. Finally Ma speaks up.

"I think what you're getting into isn't such a good idea. We're trying to make a new start, remember? You can't throw it all away. Again."

Daddy raises his voice. "I just can't sit by while some tyrant thinks he can run around dinking over guys who only want to make a living and support their families. It's not right." I start to hear the familiar rhythm of heartbeats in my ears. Fear. I wonder if Kevin and Char fight like my parents do, if Angie ever feels scared lying in bed at night.

"I know, I know," says Ma. "But what makes you

think a strike is going to make a difference? The problem is you don't know what the hell you're doing."

"Goddammit, Martha." Daddy's voice sounds harsh. Misunderstood. This is their first big fight in the new house, and it is just like all the others.

"Wayne, this is rich, you know that? You're barely on the job two weeks and you've already got a pack of asshole buddies, and not only that, you're ready to put your job on the line to go on strike? Is there nothing you won't do . . . besides the right thing?"

Last Thanksgiving I heard Grandma tell Ma that they didn't raise her to be a nomad. I stood in the hallway between the guest room and the bathroom, listening to Ma and Grandma whisper-argue about our situation. I always liked visiting my grandparents, even though Daddy complained about their fancy-pants coffeemaker that makes some kind of sludge he can't ever learn to stomach and the chairs that are not fit for a grown man to sit on. To me, their house is sunlit and clean, and I like the pictures of ballerinas and forests hung on the walls. Both Grandma and Grandpa are stylish and smart. Not at all mean and wrinkled like Daddy's mother, even though they are the same age.

I heard Ma tell Grandma she was doing just fine and things were looking up. Grandma said she begged to differ.

Ma said, "Mother, that's not fair. And here. You keep this. We're not a charity." Through the crack in the door I saw Ma push a wad of bills back at Grandma while I held my breath. I wonder if Daddy knew about that money. We could have used it.

Dishes crash in the sink.

One of them turns on the faucet. It's probably Daddy. Whenever he's really mad, he goes on a housecleaning tear. He does it to show Ma up.

That usually gets her to back down. But not this time.

"You have no idea what an idiot you're being," Ma says.

Through the open window in our bedroom I can hear the baby next door. Crying. The mother's voice goes over and over, "Shhh shhh."

Rita says, "That kid is always going off. It's a miracle anybody gets any sleep when the windows are open." Rita says this as if she hasn't heard what's happening in our own house. As if the yelling over here hadn't woken that baby up.

"You can't fix all the world's problems," Ma shouts.

My daddy's surprising generosity to people we don't know is something we all resent. I'll never forget the day Ma baked a pan of brownies and Daddy took them next door and doled them out to our neighbors. We were incredulous and hurt when he told us that we should consider ourselves lucky. We could have brownies anytime, he said, while the unfortunate neighbor kids would never know love and kindness. I hated those kids after that.

My father is obsessed with making things better, but things never work out the way he says they will, and then we move on for another fresh start. Rita thinks Ma takes too much shit from Daddy, and Toby thinks Ma doesn't cut Daddy any slack. I feel torn. I can see both sides.

Daddy's voice sounds weighted and emotional. "Martha, everything was handed to you by your parents." I don't understand why he wants her to feel guilty about that.

"Nobody up in heaven is thanking you for all the things you've screwed up down here," Ma says.

"So we're back to my brother," Daddy shoots

back, "and how I don't measure up." Daddy's brother comes up in their fights sometimes. He's a cross-country truck driver, not anybody smart or rich, so I'm not sure why.

Ma's response is acidic. "You need to think about *us*, Wayne, in the here and now. Otherwise—"

"Otherwise?" Daddy cuts her off. Daddy inhales. Ma lets her breath out. I want Rita to tell me she's scared. For once.

"I think we should split up." Ma's pronouncement makes my heart feel like stopping. I hear a rush in my ears, blood pumping a hundred miles an hour.

"Rita, did you hear that?" I whisper down to her bunk. Our parents' inability to see eye to eye has reached a breaking point. Rubberville could be the last straw.

Instead of Rita's voice I hear kitchen chair legs scraping the linoleum. She can't possibly be sleeping.

Daddy is slamming all the chairs in against the table.

"Rita?"

I hear the back door open and wheeze before it closes with a preset click.

I hear Ma weeping.

Chapter 5

ᨀ

Me and Angie are lying on her bed on our backs, listening to the "I'm in you" song, watching dust flecks drift in a beam of afternoon sunlight. Just drifting away. Perfect.

Angie rolls over toward me and touches my arm. "Libby?"

I get up on my elbows. "Yeah?"

"What are you most afraid of?"

"Swimming."

"Really? Why?"

"It's about being over my head in water. It freaks me out." When I was little, Ma and Daddy signed me up for swim class. As I stood at the edge of the pool my first day, someone pushed me in. It was such a surprise that I inhaled a lot of water and panicked when I couldn't touch bottom. The lifeguard pulled me out of the pool. Afterward, I couldn't stop coughing. Daddy wanted to have the teacher fired for her negligence. It was humiliating.

"You should try swimming with the dolphins someday," Angie says. "I saw that on TV. They help people who are afraid."

"No way," I say. The thought of them near me in the water turns my stomach.

"So what are you most afraid of?" I ask Angie in return.

She blows up at her forehead to get the hair out of her eyes. "Have you ever been . . . I don't know—"

She's interrupted when we hear a car in her driveway. Angie gets up off the bed to look out the window, disturbing the dust in the air, and then cocks her head toward mine.

Angie says to me in a whisper, "He's supposed to be at work." She stands at the side of the bed, holding her hand to her throat.

I stand up too when I hear Kevin's voice from

the kitchen. "Anyone home?"

We both look at each other, hearts skipping, and touch hands. Angie grabs my arm and pulls. "You're coming with me," she says.

Kevin yells again: "Char?"

"Libby, c'mon." Angie clutches me and pulls me up. "Now." She holds my hand as we pass through the hall, past Frankie's room, and into the kitchen.

Kevin's standing in Angie's kitchen with a carton of eggs under his arm, looking like a walking massacre. He's still wearing his work clothes, his name on a patch sewed onto his right pocket, stains radiating away from his knees. The rubber boots on his feet have little feathers stuck on them. He smells like hell.

He works at Specialty Poultry. He's on the line that slaughters the ducks. Most of the ducks don't get a chance to lay their last eggs; those get taken out during slaughter. The workers can take the eggs home and eat them if they want. Kevin brings home duck eggs by the dozen. The eggs are soft and oval, barely transparent, a milky coating over the yolk instead of a shell. Space alien eggs. Angie has to eat them. She says she can't stand to be near down coats anymore now that Kevin has brought the stink of the duck farm into her life.

He takes a drag off the cigarette hanging from the edge of his mouth and blows the smoke out of his nose toward us before saying anything.

"Take these eggs." He says "eggs" like "aches."

Angie takes the carton of eggs from him and wrinkles her nose. "You stink."

"Char home?"

"No."

"That chick is never home." Kevin frowns. "She just left you here and didn't say shit about where she was going. Right?"

"We can take care of ourselves," Angie says.

Kevin snorts. "The hell you can." He looks at me with bloodshot eyes. "What're you doing here?"

I wish I could melt into the linoleum. Angie narrows her eyes at him. "What are *you* doing here? You're supposed to be at work."

"Bring me a beer. I'll be outside." Even though he trips as he goes out the door, his body skids back into place as the screen door snaps behind him. He hunches his shoulders as he heads to the backyard.

The courtly Kevin I met a few weeks ago seems

to have been abducted by the same aliens laying the eggs.

"God, what an asshole," Angie says as she leaves the egg carton on the counter. But she obediently heads to the basement rec room. "He needs a beer like a hole in the head."

"Angie?" I follow her down to the refrigerator in the basement and tell her I should leave. She shrugs and ignores me while she opens a beer bottle with the bottle opener screwed into the wall. The "Hole in One" toe in the sock doesn't seem so funny anymore. The bottle cap falls on the cement floor. Angie kicks it toward me.

"Pick that up for me, will ya, Lib?" She takes a sip of the beer and heads back toward the stairs. I pick up the bottle cap and throw it at her head. Halfway up the stairs she turns around, shakes up the bottle to spray me with the foam. It doesn't do anything but pour down the sides of the bottle, making a mess on the stairs. She puts her mouth over the bottle top to slurp it up.

"This one's for us," she says.

I look up the stairs. "Kevin gives me beer sometimes," she says. "It's cool."

She gives me the bottle, cold and wet in my hand, the label peeling off. "C'mon, Libby. Drink up." I take a sip. I can't believe it's so bitter and terrible tasting. I keep drinking. Between chugs we wipe our mouths on our sleeves, breathing hard, passing it between us, our backs against the handrail, eyes toward the door.

"Don't leave, okay? Please."

"God, beer is gross," I say.

"I know," Angie says. "Here, you take the last swallow." She sprints back down the stairs to get Kevin his beer.

KEVIN IS SITTING in a webbed lawn chair next to the picnic table. Did he really forget that he's still wearing shit and blood? I remember Daddy said you could tell a lot about a person by the state of his shoes. His are a mess. I'd like to know why he's home in the middle of the day, but I'm not going to ask. Whenever Daddy ever showed up in the middle of the day at home, it was because he got canned. Angie motions for me to sit down. We sit across from each other at the picnic table.

"Char's got some nice roses." Kevin points at the

trellis of white roses against the house. The roses are mostly dried-up flower heads right now, but a few are still blooming, looking weird against the peeling paint of the house. Char plants things in strict rows, one petunia, two petunias, lots of room between them. To me, all her plants look lonely. Kevin likes them. He won't shut up about the roses, going on and on. "You got to be a goddamned expert to get roses that pretty," he says. "Pretty. Just like you girls. I mean it, too."

Me and Angie look at each other; we both sit up straighter.

Kevin gets up off the lawn chair, and it tips side to side before stopping upright. I barely see the knife come out of his pocket before he slices off four of Char's precious rose blooms. Not even a leaf or petal falls, just four whole heads whacked off. Kevin, beer in one hand, knife in the other, looks Angie in the eye. Then he locks eyes with me.

He whoops with laughter. "I got something to show you." I don't dare move.

He shows us the knife, a very skinny gray blade, with a black plastic handle that says NSF in upraised letters. Given the state of Kevin's clothing, I'm surprised the knife is so clean. Just a hint of green stalk on the blade where he chopped the roses. He handles the knife as if it's a piece of valuable jewelry, palms up so we can see it. The blade is permanently stained with what I'm sure are countless dead ducks.

"See, most people are scared of a knife right off. Even more than a gun. Guns are a whole different class of hardware," he says. I wouldn't know about that. I'm pretty sure I'm scared of both about equal.

"Let me give you a demonstration." I close my eyes for a second. Is Jesus my savior? Body and blood, cross my heart and hope to die? When I open them, Kevin shows us techniques interesting enough to forget about dying. One is you hold the knife upright and slash. He slashes down through the air. That's how they butcher the ducks after they've been electrocuted.

"Electrocuted?" Angie can't believe it. All this time she'd been thinking Kevin killed them by wringing their necks with his bare hands.

Another way is to grip the knife with your palm, blade facing down. That's the way you normally murder somebody. Side to side gets you the most blood. Puncture the stomach to make a point. If you mean business, go for the jugular in the neck.

"Given the kind of trouble you're likely to find yourself in, maybe a boy is trying something on you, give him the side treatment. That way you'll draw blood, get him scared, but not really hurt him too much."

I slouch down at the picnic table, feeling my muscles give way. He wants to protect us, not murder us. He wants us to like him. I should tell him he's trying too hard.

He looks around the yard for a couple of minutes and doesn't say another word. Then he gets up and picks up the roses he cut off the bush. "You girls need some flowers in your hair?" He puts one, then another behind Angie's ears. She holds her head and yelps.

"C'mon, man, those things have thorns!"

"Oh, yeah." He's a little easier on me, but not much.

I think about the Grimms' fairy tale about two sisters named after rosebushes, Snow-White and Rose-Red, who pledged that as long as they lived, they would not leave each other. "What the one has, she must share with the other," so the story goes. The girls never go anywhere without holding each other by the hand. Whenever they travel into the forest, they offer help to an ungrateful dwarf who lives in a cave. One day a bear the girls once had mercy on appears and strikes the dwarf down. The bear, having been bewitched by the dwarf, transforms into a prince, and Snow-White and Rose-Red's devotion to each other is rewarded with wealth and a long life together.

When I look at Angie, the bends at the backs of both my ears are burning with warning. She smiles at me, a strange, unhappy smile.

Chapter 6

"I didn't think you'd—" Ma says, interrupting whoever she's talking to on the phone. "You told me last night, no, promised, that you decided not to—"

The fierce warmth I felt behind my ears from Char's roses gives way to cold pins and needles. She doesn't know I'm here.

"So what should we—? Wayne. Listen to me!" Something's up with Daddy.

Even if Ma knew what just happened at Angie's, she wouldn't care.

Ma lets out this groan, and her shoulders slump against the wall by the phone. Her back is curved in toward the receiver cradled by her shoulder. She has the phone cord wrapped around her left index finger, and she is pulling it away from the wall.

From what I can gather, Daddy and some other guys tried to stop a delivery truck from coming in. They didn't do anything to the driver or the truck, just stood in its way. The cops took Daddy and some other men to jail. I could imagine Daddy standing in front of a big semi full of parts, his arms down, just standing there. Stubborn. He probably knew the driver wasn't going to run him over, but I bet he was scared just the same.

Ma hangs up before I can sneak away. She turns around and blurts out, "Your father's not coming home tonight."

I ask Ma why.

Ma lasers her eyes on mine. "Jesus Christ."

She moves her hands through her hair, gives her head a little scratch. She always acts like she has fleas whenever she doesn't want to talk about something.

Ma says what she needs right now is my help getting groceries.

She speaks to me as if I'm the one who's in trouble when I ask her again about Daddy. "Your father and the men he works with staged a wildcat sit-down. That means the men in the shop your father works with are probably not going to be working. They went on strike." This is worse than anything that's happened before. Usually Daddy loses his job, and then we move. He's never ended up in jail before.

WE BOTH SNAP out of feeling that we're in a bad dream when we walk through the automatic doors at the grocery store. It's the colors. Red apples, oranges, green things. And the grocery-store smell: meat and floor cleaner. We both grab for a cart at the same time. Ma gives me a little smile. "If I raised just one of you kids right, then I've done my job."

"Huh?" I say it the way Rita does. It just pops out.

If she knew I had been at Angie's drinking beer and watching her stepdad play with knives, I'd be in big trouble.

"Listen here, missy, if I had it in me, I'd . . ." I finish her sentence for her in my head: Leave.

Ma puts the shopping cart's seat flap up with a thump. Her eyes bulge, but she doesn't cry. I head for the produce to get away from her, look at all the leaves of lettuce ragged on the floor.

"Get over here and push this cart." I walk back to the cart, but I will never be the model daughter. Suddenly I'm glad Daddy went on strike today and that Ma doesn't care to ferret out what I did at Angie's. It's all so confusing. One minute Angie says Kevin can go to hell, but then she hurries to do his bidding. She begs me not to leave and acts afraid when he comes home, but the first day I met him, she seemed to be flirting with him. My throat hurts.

I make sure to push the cart past everything with the right speed. I count the linoleum tiles as I push the cart. They alternate white and green, white and green. I step on only the white ones. Quickly walk by the ice cream and frozen dinners, slow down at the milk and cereal. I stop the cart for a minute, put my foot on the lower rack, and wonder about Daddy, if he has his feet propped up on the bars of his cell.

As I wait for Ma, I linger a moment over the meat display. Each thing in here is a dead animal somebody had to electrocute and butcher. I watch Ma check on the price of a roast; she throws ground beef in the cart instead. Every week she buys five pounds of hamburger on a Styrofoam tray and divides it into five one-pound blobs, wraps each in a single layer of waxed paper, and tosses it in the freezer. We have chicken on the weekends.

"Beats me how we're going to afford to eat," she says. "Of course they rely on that to keep people from— It's a damned-if-you-do, damned-if-you-don't situation."

We make our way through the grocery, avoiding the minefields of high prices. I don't beg for a single thing, not even a candy bar at the checkout.

When we get home, the morning's dishes are still piled up in the sink, so Ma fills it with scalding water and dish soap. Before I can sneak away, Ma asks for my help washing the dishes. She asks in a nice way. She doesn't even check to see if I'm putting the groceries away properly.

Ma glances out the window toward the Foxy Lady van. Sometimes I think she sends secret little prayers out to it. Her right hand holds a seasoned wooden cooking spoon. She doesn't bother to portion out the hamburger for the freezer, just plops the whole thing in a pan. She starts stirring vigorously, flipping and scraping the meat over and over, bearing down on the edge of the spoon to break the chunk apart. I imagine that's what she's doing with her thoughts. If you ever ask Ma what she's going to make for dinner, she'll say, "Oh, I don't know." And she doesn't. Sometimes she jokes about tying it up with a string and pouring wine on it. Maybe she's thinking about cooking a pot roast that she'll present to the family, instead of what we're really having.

MA ANNOUNCES TO everyone at dinner that we all have to pitch in. The sound of our forks on plates stops. For a second we hear Ma's breathing, see the rise and fall of her chest moving. None of us is really used to her saying something like that, that from now on we are going to change. Those are Daddy's lines.

"That's what Daddy says every time we get ready to leave," Rita says. The idea we might move sends a shiver of panic through me. I want to leave Rubberville, but not Angie. Not now.

Ma sighs when she looks at Rita. Rita sits at the table like a movie star, haughty and mysterious. She wears a clingy shirt, short shorts, and these three-inch platform heels. Her makeup is beautiful and rowdy-looking. They already had a big fight last week about the shoes. Ma said they were too strappy and revealing of her toes. I'm pretty sure when she goes out, nobody is looking at her feet.

Ma says that this is not about moving but staying. I don't believe her.

Toby says, "Knock it off, Rita—everything's not all about your little life." Toby says he's proud of Daddy for standing up to the big guys like that. It's about time after his getting kicked around all these years.

Ma's voice sounds hoarse. "But you have to remember that we're not going to have his paycheck. We'll need you kids to—" I realize she's trying to get us to see her side of things, that the strike might be the thing that breaks us apart. "We'll just have to tighten our belts for a little while," she says.

Nobody knows what to say, and nobody eats any more either.

"The strike is a last resort, if there is no other way to get fairness," Daddy said the night all the men were here.

Ma says, "It's important for us to support Daddy." She looks down at her lap and picks at her fingers.

Rita says she'd be happy to go out and picket.

"A picket line is no place for a young lady, Rita," Ma says.

Rita replies, "I want to help."

"You'll do what I say," Ma says. As if saying this will stop Rita.

I look at Rita and narrow my eyes. She flips me the finger under the table.

After dinner, Carl and a couple of men I've never seen before from the plant stop by to see if we need anything. Ma looks flattened, smoothing down the wrinkles on her polyester pants, her fingernails bitten to the quick.

"Oh, we're fine. He'll be home tomorrow." Ma steadies herself, doesn't forget her manners, even though I'm sure she'd like them to leave. Carl takes her offered cup of coffee. One of the men says working the line would make anybody crazy, what with speedups and then layoffs. A trip to the icehouse on behalf of the cause is noble. They will take care of it; they will help out. Ma's smile never changes.

After the men leave, we hear the sound of something hitting the front of our house. Something thrown. Toby leaves the table and rushes outside even though Ma yells at him to leave it be. Me and Rita reach toward each other, put our hands together, and look at each other. Without saying anything, we know. This is definitely about having to leave. Toby comes back inside carrying a brick that has a piece of paper attached to it with a rubber band. "Hey, Ma," Toby says, breathing hard, "I think they missed their target. I bet they wanted this to go through the window." The notebook paper attached to the brick is yellow with blue lines on it. It has one word written on it: STOP.

Chapter 7

Angie is using some contraption that looks like it will yank out her eyelashes. "It's an eyelash curler," she says. She takes the thing off her lashes and says, "See," and bats her eyes at me. Then she starts to put all kinds of eye makeup on, black liner and blue shadow.

"I need a new look," she says.

Angie turns toward all these little pots of lip gloss and trays of blush and eye shadow sitting on the sink's vanity. I try to shrug off the feeling that maybe she stole all that makeup, that she has to hide things about herself from me.

Apart from the polish on my own nail-bitten fingers, I've never worn any of this stuff. Angie looks pretty good.

I remind her it's almost the end of July and ask her about the sidewalk sale with the pony rides. Angie smirks and turns back to the mirror. I lean against the vanity, careful not to knock anything off. I roll up the Arabian horse magazine I brought over and place it at my feet. We'll look at it later.

Angie grabs a compact with blush in it. Very pink. She sucks in her cheeks and applies the color to the hollows. She explains that if you put the color on your cheekbones, you'll get the clown effect. It's good she's telling me. That's exactly where I'd have put it.

The light overhead in the bathroom seems too bright, even though Angie complains she can't see shit. "I'm gonna get me one of those Clairol mirrors." I know the one she's talking about, where you can change the light on it from day to night and flip the mirror around for a close-up view.

Angie pushes some lipstick tubes toward me. She makes me feel like I've never done a glamorous thing in my entire life. I know it is time to change that, but how? I uncap the tubes and run a few streaks of different lip colors on the inside of my arm. I've seen Rita do that at stores; she says it's how you tell what would look good on your face. To me they all look good, both the light and shimmery ones and the deeply colored ones. I take one tube and gently run it over my lips. It feels waxy. The whole time I'm trying on the lipstick, I keep my eyes on Angie in the mirror. I want her reaction. I want to start high school with a whole new look.

Angie doesn't comment on the lipstick; she says my pores are large. I need an astringent to close them up, she says.

I sit down on the toilet seat lid and rest my feet on the edge of the tub.

There are damp towels on the floor and a crumpled rug in need of shaking out. Toilet paper is stacked on a plunger handle next to the tank. In between a mix of scissors, tweezers, and a little round radio are combs on a shelf with a bunch of bottles, some a little battered-looking. Char's got a thing for lotion. Same for shampoo. Five different brands on the tub's ledge. Even baby shampoo. Nobody here has been a baby for a good long time.

I breathe in and out slowly as Angie rubs astringent

over my forehead and into the place where my nose meets my upper lip. The astringent feels cool and refreshing. Hope rises in my chest. Angie's singing along with a song on the radio. " 'It's a beautiful day,' " she sings softly, off-key. " 'Don't let it get away'— I love this song," she says.

"What was up with Kevin the other day when I was over? He seemed, I don't know, drunk or something," I say.

"He gets like that," she says. She acts like what happened is no big deal.

Angie shows me the dirt on the cotton ball from my face. "That's why you do this, Libby." She tells me to stand up and look in the mirror and see how my pores are smaller now.

"They look the same," I say. Angie shrugs. I wipe off the lipstick I have on with the back of my hand. The redness smudged into my skin looks like a wound.

She says, "It's your turn, Libby. Do something cute with my hair."

"Angie . . ."

"C'mon. It'll be fun."

I hand her the horse magazine I brought over

while she sits on the toilet lid. I thought Angie and I both loved horses more than anything. That's what I thought originally inspired her to paint the horse picture for me. I still want a horse, but now I think she'd rather have a makeup mirror.

"You do need a new hairstyle," I tell her. "Your hair is kind of dorky right now. Nobody wears barrettes on top of their head anymore."

It sounds like something she would say to me. Even though I can't see her face, I know I'm getting to her.

I pile her hair into a tight ponytail at the top of her head. "I'm giving you the Alien Rocker," I say. I grab a can of Char's hair spray. "Don't worry. It'll wash out," I say to Angie. I tease her hair into a poof.

I make the ponytail tighter.

"Hey, don't rip my hair out."

"You want a new hairstyle or not?"

"Libby, that hair spray makes me want to throw up." Angie tries to get up off the toilet seat.

"Sit still."

I take down the ponytail and pull sections of her hair in my hands. Angie's hair is very fine, and with all the hair spray it feels tacky.

"Okay, but look." Angie points to an Arabian stallion in the horse magazine, his long mane sectioned into braids with ribbon woven into the strands. "Do this to my hair."

"Don't move," I say. Something mean flares up inside me. I comb her hair out and over her eyes.

"You've been wearing your hair the same way *since you were born.*"

Slowly I reach over her head to the pile of tweezers, scissors, and fingernail clippers on the shelf. I pick up the scissors without a sound.

I slide the scissors under her hair and make one long cut, the shears making a dull metal sound against her head. I let go of her, and a foot of hair sails to the floor.

"Libby! What the hell!" Angie's one makeup-darkened eye glares at me as she jumps up off the toilet seat. She cuffs me a good one on the right side of my head. I drop the scissors on the floor. My eyes are watering, and I can't breathe. I put up my arms to shield myself when she slams me against the wall.

The blow brings me back to my old self. I hold my breath for a moment and let it out when Angie turns away from me to look at herself in the mirror.

I laugh at her shock.

"God, Libby, it's not funny," she says.

"I just thought you'd really kill me."

"I should," she says. But as she looks at herself in the mirror, she sees potential for this new hairdo right away. She pulls her hair up and down, rolls her shoulders, and pouts at the mirror. It makes her look older, more grown-up.

I tell her if we wet it down, I can get a better cut. I spit on the comb and run it through Angie's new bangs and make a couple more cuts. I still can't see her eyes too well, so I cut again. Another inch of hair falls away from her face. She looks pleased.

ANGIE SAYS I should look at more than just horse magazines all the time. It's time I grew up, she says. We go to her room, where she shows me a stack of some magazines she says Kevin gave her.

We listen to records and lie on her bed looking at *Playboy* and *Hustler*. I've seen them before, at a few places Ma cleans, but she always shoos me off. Now I can see what the big deal is. We're looking at a lady with big boobs taking a shower, one hand between her legs. The woman's body is wet and soapy.

"I have to tell you something," Angie says. Her voice is quiet, her face doubly serious framed by her shorter new hairdo.

Angie waits a heartbeat, while I hang my breath on it.

She says that the time has come to tell me the truth, because I was starting to put two and two together.

"Angie . . ." I wonder what the truth could be. Whatever it is, I have a feeling I don't want to know. "Hey." I point right away to another picture of a woman in a magazine with a guy who looks like Zorro. "I'm sure she's just going to sit there and let that guy blindfold her," I say sarcastically.

"Why not? That, and a bunch of other things too. Kevin said life is all about"— she takes the magazine away from me and turns the page—"giving in to—" She points to a word. "XXTACY."

"Kevin said that?"

She sees the shocked look on my face and says, "Libby, you know what? Sometimes you act like you are so above it."

"Above what?"

I want to say her stepdad probably shouldn't give

her these magazines to look at, but I don't say it.

"God, Libby. Take a look at this." I look.

"Made you look, you dirty crook." Then she howls like a wolf. "You crack me up."

She opens all the magazines and lays them out in a row on the bed. She points to a girl with gigantic boobs. Angie says we need to start thinking up new names for ourselves. "I think the name Libby is fine if you're just going to be boring the rest of your life."

"How about Nikki?"

Nikki is playmate of the month, and she measures 40-26-34. She prefers kittens to puppies and loves long walks on the beach.

Angie sits up straight on the bed and looks at me for a second. "You need to loosen up."

Angie gets up off the bed and reaches for a CD and plops it in the player. A scratchy voice inches its way around the room. The song sounds round, shimmery.

She rolls up my old purple T-shirt from our shirt trade and throws it over her shoulder, pretending it's a feather boa. To be a real stripper, you have to have one, she explains. She jumps up on the bed to give herself a bigger stage and tells me to sit on the floor.

The open magazines bounce along but miraculously don't fall off the bed. She turns her back to me, then rolls her shoulders and works the T-shirt down her back. She gets it down to her butt and moves it back and forth across her behind. Then she twirls the "feather boa" over her head. She flings it at me from between her legs. I say, "Watch where you're throwing that." She laughs and pulls her shirt over her head. She shimmies her shoulders, and her boobs bounce a little in her bra as she springs up and down on the bed. She turns away from me and unhooks her bra. Then she turns around. Her boobs are so white and flatter than I thought they were.

"C'mon. I dare you to try it," Angie says to me, a little breathless. "Just go ahead and take your top off to the music. The song's almost over!" Angie puts her top back on and throws my old T-shirt toward me. "Here's your feather boa." I stand up. I look down at the zebra rug pattern, avoiding the pictures of naked women on the bed, and feel a little dizzy.

My mouth and my limbs are having trouble moving. "Hey sailor," I say shyly, and give a little kick like I imagine a real stripper would. I run my hands up and down my legs, my shoulders. Angie sits on the bed and sticks her tongue out at me. I look away through her bedroom window to the picnic table in the backyard.

Ma is always telling me stuff like: "Keep your legs crossed, hands to yourself, be an example." It's not like I've ever done anything she needs to worry about. I start to unbutton my shirt, but the song is almost over. Angie puts her hand over her mouth. So far I wouldn't get a pack of gum for my striptease act. I have not shown a single body part. I get up on the bed with Angie and jump up and down to get some rhythm going and put my hands behind my back.

I can't bring myself to take anything off. Angie turns the music off. I sit down on the edge of her bed, and she sits on the floor on the zebra rug. I think she's mad I'm not going along.

Angie's eye makeup is smudged and raccoony. She's been rubbing her eyes because her new bangs fall into them. Angie puts her arm around my right leg, and does spider dances with her fingers on my feet, then turns away from me and picks up a brush and starts brushing her hair. I get down off the bed and sit on the floor next to her.

We don't say anything to each other for a long time. I listen to Angie's breathing. Birds banter, and a car with a roaring motor drives by. Its muffler must've fallen off.

Angie flips open another *Penthouse,* and a smaller magazine tucked between the pages falls out. This one is different. This one is all black-and-white photos, one after another, of ordinary-looking girls. Except here they're totally naked, and some are young, like us. In one, an older guy is bent over a girl from behind, seeming to push into her. In another, a girl with a flat chest sits on a man's lap with her legs spread apart. We flip the pages briskly, our breaths practically moving the pages for us. These girls could be anybody we know. I wonder out loud why anyone would want to look at this. Angie swallows, says she doesn't know. I look at my friend. Suddenly it seems as if all the things we've ever said or done together before were childish. I feel a sting of shame in my throat that keeps me from saying anything else.

Chapter 8

❧

M a pulls down the visor on her side of the car to cut down the glare from the late-afternoon sun and hits the gas. She's driving a little too fast for this neighborhood, and I see the lake flash between houses. Brick house. Blue lake. House. Lake. Over and over. I put my arm out the window and feel the breeze. I've been helping her clean today, and the fresh air feels good. Ma looks at me, and her face softens. Then she turns her attention back to her driving.

My mouth moves without my brain, and I blurt, "Ma, do you think a girl could fall in love with a guy who made her do . . . things?"

"What kind of things?" Ma asks. The dreamy look on her face has evaporated, and her forehead wrinkles. She hits the brakes a little too hard at the stop sign.

"Things like . . ." Ma's eyes are bugged out and focused on my face, willing herself to understand my question. Her eyes narrow. "Libby?"

I'm suddenly burning hot. I focus on the car's dashboard, all the dials, the speedometer that goes to 110, willing myself to forget Angie's bare chest, why she didn't want me to leave that day when Kevin got home early. "Nothing," I reply.

"Libby." Ma puts her hand under my chin. The black-and-white pictures of the girls I saw in the magazine at Angie's somersault through my mind, one after the other.

"Libby?" Ma's concern is overwhelming. Her eagerness to know what I'm talking about makes my hands sweat. I leave little wet handprints on the car seat while Ma waits for an answer.

"You know, like what happened on that one TV show? Could you fall in love with the guy after that?" The man had forced himself on the main character, but then she fell in love with him. I congratulate myself on thinking fast without actually lying.

I'm stifling in the heat, trying not to faint from the potency of my mother's concerned confusion.

Ma breathes in. Her chest falls in relief. "Nobody would fall in love after that. Not in real life," she replies.

I think of the movie on the facts of life I saw back in fifth grade. We had to have a permission slip to see it, and mothers could be there if they wanted to.

Ma couldn't be there but said she'd be right there to pick me up after school and we could talk about it afterward. I never knew a single movie could be so important.

The day of the movie all the fifth-grade girls, excited to finally learn about the secrets of womanhood, were taken to the auditorium. The girls bobbed their heads and swayed toward one another, not ready to settle down. The lunchroom monitors helped the teachers try to shut everyone up.

The girl in the seat next to me told me she already knew everything she needed to know and that the movie was for babies who didn't know jack shit. I pulled my sweater closer to my chest. I could not pretend. I didn't know jack shit. The mothers who came sat in the back rows and looked concerned about the goings-on the movie inspired well before anybody saw it.

There were actually two movies. The first was about the insides of a girl and the insides of a boy. The girl's reproductive system had tubes and an egg and a lining that peeled off once a month. Her period! After I saw that, I hoped I'd never get one, but I ended up getting it just the same.

In the second movie there was a cartoon of a man entering a woman and then releasing the millions of little tadpoles that would swim toward her one and only egg. Those little tadpoles would eat away at the egg until one got in. The movie showed a cartoon *penis* that went into the girl's *vagina* and released its *sperm*; a lot of little squiggles took over the screen. When the sperm met the egg, they pecked at it until *boom*, one got in and you made a baby. I had no idea. No idea at all. It seemed like the last thing I'd let anybody do to me.

After the movies the nurse handed out these little blue books that said PERSONALLY YOURS on the cover and had more pictures of a girl's reproductive system.

One of the teachers, a young one with bright red lipstick and a fashionable scarf tied around her neck, said she would speak frankly and said that it was important to use the correct terminology for things. A woman had a vagina, and a man had a penis, not a pussy and a dick. A girl had a period; a "friend" was not visiting. People did not fuck; they had sexual intercourse. She showed us a tampon, which she held in the air for all to see as she talked about being clean. She talked about being a lady. The nurse nodded in agreement. You could have heard a pin drop in that auditorium. The girl who said she knew everything sat next to me with her mouth open. The mothers in back looked flushed. The whole thing was just too much. When it was over, I pulled up my drooping knee socks and knew why Ma wanted to see me afterward.

When she picked me up, Ma asked me if I had any questions. She said if I ever wanted to talk about anything, anything personal, I should feel free to ask her anything. That day I thought about the boy who told me he liked me and stole milk containers for me at lunch. I wondered if his actions were part of what this movie was talking about. I didn't know how to ask without admitting to being party to a crime, so I didn't say anything.

I run my hand over the scorching hot vinyl of the car's front seat, thinking about the lunchroom boy, and Angie's striptease, Kevin's knife techniques, the magazines.

I think about a scene I saw recently on TV, where a woman greeted this guy and ran her hands over the back of his neck and shoulders. Then she tickled him a little and put her fingers along the waistband of his pants. Could that be happening between Angie and Kevin?

Ma gets straight to the point. "Libby, I want you to know I'm willing to talk about anything."

I believe she's saying this because she thinks she should. It's from a script on modern motherhood. She's really not that open, but she wants to be.

I feel the same expectation and tension I felt that day back in elementary school. I decide to change the subject a little. Everything has just been too much.

"Who was the boy who kissed you first, Ma?"

"Your father." Oh.

"How did you meet Daddy?" It seems weird I've never asked. I'd always thought of Ma and Daddy as if they were giants who met at the top of a beanstalk.

Ma breaks out a smile at the memory. She said Daddy was working on a crew doing maintenance at a park in Chicago near her parents' house. He was fixing a fence around a flower bed near the bench she was sitting on. "He looked handy with pliers." She said they got to talking as he worked. "About the weather, of all things," Ma says, "and I just fell for him. The way he felt about the sun and the rain. It was as simple as that." Her hand rubs the steering wheel.

Ma says "simple," but I don't think it's ever been simple. I know none of my grandparents liked the idea of their being together. Each set of parents hoped Ma or Daddy would come to their senses and it would be over. She must've been in love, to defy her parents and reject all they had planned for her.

Ma's been acting as if there's nothing wrong with our family, but her face has become more rigid lately, and she seems to be sucking in her cheeks all the time. Ever since Daddy got out of jail on bond last week, she also hasn't said a word about the strike.

Instead she's been nagging Daddy about staying "productive." At dinner last night Daddy told her to go to hell. As simple as that. As simple as falling in love in the first place.

Blood rockets through my ears, and I hear my pulse. Except for Angie, Rubberville has pretty much gone the way of every other place we've ever lived.

Ma shifts her bottom to keep her thighs from sticking to the driver's seat. She keeps both hands on the wheel and waits for me to say something, but I suddenly feel tired. I keep quiet all the rest of the way home.

Chapter 9

Angie calls to tell me it's time to help with the pony rides. When I'm with the ponies, my doubts about Kevin fade. I can forget about what happened after I cut Angie's hair and she danced with her top off. At the pony rides, I can go back to believing dreams can come true.

For three days we get to do everything. When the ponies poop in the straw during the pony ride circle, we run out there and scoop it up. When it's time to put the kids on and take them off the rides, we're there showing them how to put their feet in the stirrups, buckling them in the saddle, even if they're big kids our age. We try to convince the little ones to hold on to the saddle horn and not pull on the mane. No kicking or bouncing. A lot of times we have to wait to start the ride because someone needs a picture taken. When the ride starts, me and Angie walk the circle with the ponies, just to make sure everything is okay. There's not a speck of shade out in the Elmwood Plaza parking lot, so this is hard work.

My pony, Sally No, smells like a sour green apple, and she's just as tart. The people who own her, the Simons, are always saying Sally No this, Sally No that, every time that little pony moves. I love everything about her. She's a little taller than the other ponies. She's dappled brown, with a cropped black mane and long tail. Her nose is soft as a baby's butt. She stands with her back right leg cocked. I'm never sure if she's going to haul off and kick, with big plans to bolt, or if she's just resting, one leg at a time. Sally No flicks her tail, and I come running. Does she need water? Oats? Brushing? A pat?

Angie's in love with Not Sally, another brown one. She's so tame, the Simons always give her the tiny kids or the scared ones. If some kid starts out the ride bawling, pulling on the reins too hard, she just slows to practically a crawl. That makes Sally No crazy, because if Not Sally goes slow, all the other ponies have to go the same pace. Sally No wants to run, pulling her head up and down over the bar she's chained to, keeping her and the other horses going around and around in the same circle all day. I tell Sally No she's a beautiful girl, a tough girl, that she doesn't have to do anything she doesn't want to do. Usually after a couple of go-rounds, the kid shuts up, and Not Sally picks up the pace. She's a very good pony too.

Angie will never wipe a dish or fold a speck of laundry, but I've never seen her work so hard as she does around these horses. She carries heavy buckets of water for the ponies to drink from and will brush Not Sally till you can practically see your face reflected in her coat. She doesn't even complain that her arms are ready to fall off. Her tenderness around the ponies makes me wonder what Angie would be like if she didn't always have to be so tough. "Real love is horse love," she says. I couldn't agree more.

Angie even checks Not Sally's teeth and looks at her hooves to make sure no stones get under the shoes. She's trying to prevent a tragedy like the one in *Black Beauty* where the horse split a hoof and was ruined because of a stone that a drunken groom didn't notice. The people who run the rides just about turned pure white under their straw hats and checkered scarves when they saw Angie bend down to inspect Not Sally's hooves. She did it right, though, standing with her body the opposite of kicking direction, holding the hoof with both hands supported by her knee. I was surprised she'd been paying attention when I'd told her how you do it.

"Hey, kid, careful there. I think the pony is fine. Last thing I need is for someone to come down here and shut us down." Mrs. Simon turns away. "Damn kid'll get her head bashed in." Mrs. Simon's a little tense about us. Mr. Simon isn't. He seems glad to have us scoop shit; besides, there are risks other than our getting kicked by a pony or being shut down. Danny, for instance. He's their son and the one who named our ponies Sally No and Not Sally.

The Simons have a miniature stagecoach, pulled by a couple of ponies not in the pony ride circle. It's brown paneled with a little fake dust painted on the doors. Stenciled above the tiny doors are the words PONY EXPRESS. From the other end of the parking lot it's believable. Up close it's not much. Even Cinderella wouldn't want it to come at midnight. I'd much rather ride in the Foxy Lady van.

The stagecoach is only about as tall as Danny, but it seems to fit all the kids who are dying to ride in it. Danny's the driver, guiding the ponies as they pull the coach around and around the parking lot. I've seen cars pull into the parking lot, barely missing the stagecoach right in front of them while Danny pulls on the reins, going, "Whoa." Half the time those people don't even notice there's an event. Someday that stagecoach will bump out of control over a store's sidewalk curb, take out some bins, and run over some snooty saleslady. Mr. and Mrs. Simon have their hands full on Sidewalk Sale Days.

FOUR TIMES A day the ponies get to take a break. We unhook them from the big wheel that keeps them going in circles and lead them to the shade by their horse trailers. That's where we brush them, give them some food and water, and get to know every cowlick and knob on their hair. We take off their saddles, rub clean rags over the tooled leather to remove finger-prints, and fluff the damp saddle blankets. Then I grab a currycomb and start brushing Sally No. She relaxes with the handling and stands patient, her back right hoof cocked. I spread my arms over Sally No's girth, rest my cheek against her stomach, and listen to her breathe. I feel her blood pumping millimeters away from my own. Heaven. If we could keep Sally No and Not Sally somewhere, anywhere, stabled in Angie's garage or pastured in my backyard, everything would be perfect.

Danny sits on a hay bale, smoking and watching me and Angie. We put up with him for the sake of the Sallys. He's skinny and zitty, with long blond hair he keeps tucked under a felt cowboy hat. He doesn't wear a checkered scarf or straw hat like his parents. He wears a rock band T-shirt with men wearing heavy makeup on it. It's hard to tell how old Danny is. Is he a grown man or not? "He ain't no Marlboro Man, that's for sure," says Angie. We hate him, in part because he has no idea how lucky he is, surrounded by ponies all his life.

"Danny. Put out the damn cigarette. I've told you and told you. No smoking around the horses." Mr. Simon's face is redder than ever. Danny looks at Mr. Simon as if he's just met some crazy person.

He does what he's told, after he's taken a huge drag and blown out some smoke rings. His lips look ready to break. The O's come out in silent defiance. The ponies don't even blink.

"These girls sure are horse crazy. The worst case I've ever seen. Don'tcha think?" He laughs. Mrs. Simon looks at us and shrugs; her face is a pudgy sphere of concern and stinginess.

I stroke Sally No's forehead, trying to ignore him.

Without a cigarette, Danny starts talking and won't shut up. "Hey, how'd you girls like to do this full-time? You know, bake out in the sun, cleaning horseshit out of trailers, being at shopping centers half your life?" Mr. Simon should let him have another cigarette, just to shut him up.

"I would." I don't say it too loud, but I'd do anything to have a life like his.

WE HELP SADDLE the ponies for the next session. Mr. Simon inspects our work and cinches each saddle tighter, putting a knee into each pony's belly.

"See, here's the problem." He explains how the ponies will fill themselves with air when they get saddled. It's a little trick they do to keep you from knowing the saddle's not on tight. I watch Mr. Simon give Sally No a good dig with his knee. "Don't worry, Libby, it don't hurt," he says when he sees the look on my face. Sally No deflates. Mr. Simon's fingers nimbly cinch the saddle. "Like that. Next time I'll let you try it. But it takes some practice. Shetlands are crafty little buggers."

Once the pony rides get going again, a lady shows up with a real little kid, a girl in a blinding white sunsuit. Mr. Simon takes care of that one and puts her on Not Sally. I stand at the edge of the pony circle, holding the bar that keeps Sally No in place. The paint is flaking off in spots, and I chip off a little more while I wait, getting a yellow piece stuck under my fingernail. The girl sits atop Not Sally like a drop of whipped cream with eyes. Mr. Simon gives Not Sally a friendly slap on the rump to get the ride going. Angie starts to move the pole Not Sally is attached to. Not Sally won't move. The other kids start kicking their ponies to get the ride going. Mr. Simon unbuckles the child and hands her over to the mother.

"Sorry, ma'am," he says. The girl's mother tries to hand her back, says to Mr. Simon, "Just go ahead.

She'll get used to it." That's okay for her to say, but Not Sally won't budge. When they pull her off the pony, the little girl throws a tantrum as if she's just got told about the real Santa. Not Sally goes around without a rider this time, and Angie smiles at me as we listen to the girl's screams die out. If these were our ponies, nobody but us would ride them.

The rest of the day we see lots of tears, kids over-tired from getting dragged around the Elmwood Plaza. The shopping center is huge, usually half empty and tarred black with door after door of stores and outdoor displays, all out in the sun. Hot, hot, hot.

Some kids ride the ponies over and over again, getting back in line after their turns are over. Me and Angie try to do something about it, telling them they've had enough, but the Simons don't seem to care, letting the same kids on and off all afternoon. If Sally No were mine, I'd ride her all around the parking lot and up and down my block, not tied up to some bar that goes in circles all day. Some other ponies clop by, pulling the stagecoach. Six kids are inside; they wave at us as they pass.

Mrs. Simon says to me and Angie she doesn't want any sunstroke victims on her hands. She gives us a few dollars and tells us to go. "Skedaddle, girls," she says, waving her hands.

ALL THE STORES have stuff outside, scorching away in the late-July heat, hanging deadlocked from racks on the sidewalk. We're reminded over and over again not to touch a thing with our grimy horse hands as we pass.

Angie stops to arrange her hair in the reflection of a store window. "Can you believe Kevin freaked out on my new haircut? I think it looks cool." She won't tell me exactly what happened, but I've seen the four little bruises on her arm under her T-shirt sleeve.

I feel shame creep over me.

Angie looks away from herself toward me. "You need a good bra, Libby. The one you got on ain't working. We should go to the mall. Soon."

We finally get to the diner and sit at the counter. The stool's silver-flecked vinyl seat is cool, and it feels good. The backs of my legs warm it up quick, though, and I end up sticking to my seat. The ladies who work behind the counter have nets over their hair and drawn-on eyebrows. Our waitress tells us she wants to see our money before taking our order. We hold out horsy hands revealing limp bills and warm coins. I feel like throwing my money at her. "See," I say to her. Angie nods. The fake eyebrows knit together. The waitress doesn't say a word, just turns and starts peeling two bananas. Tomorrow is the last day the ponies will be here.

I swivel on my seat in the direction Angie's pointing. It's Danny. Today's T-shirt has on it these naked blond girls climbing a set of stairs. Mostly you notice their bare behinds.

Danny heads straight for the stool next to mine. He takes his hat off as if, being indoors around ladies, he's minding his manners. His hair falls to his shoulders in dull clumps. I want to ask him to put the hat back on. Angie makes an audible ugh sound. I elbow her.

"Hello, girls. Working up a sweat today, I see." His arms look like rods as he puts his elbows on the counter, running his hands through his hair. His fingernails are caked in half-moons of dirt. Eyebrow Pencil smiles at him, takes his order for a grilled cheese, and doesn't ask to see his money before giving the cook the order ticket.

He waves to the waitress. "Ma'am? Whatever these two are having, put it on my bill." That's a switch. Danny shifts a blue-jeaned leg toward me. "Time to celebrate. After tomorrow, I'm gone. No more horseshit for me." He doesn't seem to notice we have not said a word to him. Not even thank you.

"Next week they'll be down in Kenosha for some lakefront celebration crap. I can't wait to miss that." Danny smirks. "Hey, how come you haven't been up to see me on the coach yet? Too busy lovin' up on them ponies?"

"Why are you leaving them?" I ask.

"Are you kidding? You kill me, you know that?" His sandwich arrives, cheese melting out from under the toasted bread, the pickle showing signs of age, dangling at the edge of the plate.

Angie speaks. "Danny, are you always so . . . weird?"

"As weird as you are." Danny crooks a finger as if to chuck it under my chin.

"Hey, quit messing with her," Angie says. Then she pushes her sleeves up and shows him her muscles. When she flexes her arm, I see the green, evenly spaced bruises above her biceps. I wish I could melt into the floor.

Danny shrugs, and says, "Not impressed, kiddo." We all go back to being quiet.

Then he tells us about how they're always looking for riders down in Kentucky, someone to walk the thoroughbreds. Danny's voice drops in tone as he says the people who walk racehorses to cool them down between practice heats are called hot-walkers.

"A hot-walker," I whisper to Angie. "I never even heard of that." Sounds like streetwalker. I know Angie's thinking the same thing.

I ask Danny, "So, what do hot-walkers do exactly?"

He looks us both in the eye, but then he looks at me a second or two longer, as if I already know the answer. His voice is still, a near whisper so the waitresses won't hear. "Well, their job is to help out with racehorses. Thoroughbreds. You don't just walk them; you ride them too. Maybe spend the night with them in their stall to keep them company if they're nervous types. Depends." Danny slaps a ketchup bottle's bottom in the air before spilling a blob on his plate.

I want to ask about how a person could get to do

a job like that, but it's Danny I'm talking to, not somebody I trust.

But after he finishes his sandwich, I can't stop myself. I ask him how I can get to be a hot-walker. He just laughs. In my mind I've already run away to Kentucky when Angie grabs my elbow and pulls me off my stool so fast, the backs of my legs are burning as if someone's pulled giant Band-Aids off them.

"What makes you think she'd go anyway?" she barks at Danny.

THE LAST DAY of the pony rides is like the others: There're the crying kids, the same kids we've seen since the sidewalk sale started, and another rock T-shirt beams out from Danny's sunken chest. The ponies go around and around their little patch of parking lot. The stagecoach goes around and around the Elmwood Plaza, each near miss bringing Danny or some innocent bystander closer to God. Everything in the universe revolves around the unrelenting sun of the Sidewalk Sale Days, and when it's over, things will go back indoors away from the glare. And me and Angie will go back to buying our own banana splits. We'll hear the familiar tune of change clinking quietly in cash register drawers, mild elevator music, hangers that whisper along metal racks as shoppers take the time to choose and compare, without the heat and worry of finding the cheapest things.

"Oh, my God. Look at this. Are you girls too much or what? Angie, honey, look at you." It's Char. She points toward Angie for the benefit of those in line waiting for the pony rides to start again. "That's my baby, working herself to death over that little pony."

I never thought Angie's mother would end up at Sidewalk Sale Days. She's not much of a shopper. Angie says she likes to spend her days having drinks with ice cubes, smoking, or playing music and dancing—if she's home.

I've never seen Char outside. Her skin is blotched with the blur of too much booze; her long sprayed hair falls into her big brown eyes, all made up. Mrs. Simon's antennae go up, and she homes in, working her way toward the ponies.

Angie's mother is scaring the bejesus out of her.

"Ma'am, is there a problem?"

"There's my baby slaving away for you people.

She loves it, though. Guess I can't stop her. I came to bring her some lunch." She shakes a brown bag right in front of Mrs. Simon's face as if a certain someone ought to know why a certain concerned parent would stop by. She flips the bag to Angie, who can't pretend her mother isn't here anymore and saunters over. Angie opens the bag. We both look inside. Peanuts in their shells, and that's it.

"Well, look at that." Char stops dead in front of the stagecoach. "Is that the most precious thing you've ever seen? Where in the world did you people find this thing? Munchkinland?" She steps around to view the other side of it, where she finds Danny hiding, smoking a cigarette.

"Ma'am?" he says, more question than greeting.

Char hightails it back around. "Who is that boy there?"

Mrs. Simon says, "My son." Her continually pinched face doesn't change.

"He's kinda cute, huh, girls?" She winks at me. I'm not sure who she's insulting.

"See, I brought my camera." She dangles it by its strap above her head. She turns to Mrs. Simon. "When girls as sweet as these give their hearts to horses, you gotta record that moment for all time."

Char points her camera at Angie and Not Sally. "Honey, are you doing something different with your hair?" Char has finally noticed she's got bangs. Has she seen Kevin's fingerprints on Angie's arm? I feel as if someone has just put an ice cube down my back.

Char snaps a photo of me with Sally No and another of Angie with Not Sally.

"I'm not done, though. I need you girls to get up on that stagecoach."

"Mom . . ." Angie holds Not Sally's head, strokes her forelock absently. Neither of us can fathom saying good-bye to our ponies. Char is reminding us the ponies will become history.

Char points her camera at the stagecoach. "Ready!"

"You should tell her no," I whisper to Angie.

"We can't let her just stand there," says Angie, and she puts her fingers in my palm and gently leads me toward the stagecoach.

Danny's already up on the driver's bench, un-invited, grinning down at us. We arrange ourselves on the seat without his offered help, one on either side of him because he won't move over or leave. He puts an arm around each of us and says, "That's better, don'tcha think?"

Char frames us together in her shot. Danny's callused fingers curl around my bare shoulder after the picture is snapped. He says, "I think I like you better. You're sweet as punch." My skin and brain divide, subtracting his touch.

Chapter 10

I look out the living room window at our front-yard sidewalk sloping down toward the curb and the Foxy Lady van parked out there. Her painted face, constant smile, and flowing hair now feel like part of an ordinary day in Rubberville. Across the street at Angie's, a screen flaps out of the aluminum front door. I lean toward the window to get a better look.

At our last house there were no other things to look at, just pine trees and red-brown dirt in the long driveway. I'd stare at that drive till my eyes crossed, praying for people to drive up and keep us in the worm business. The air there was close and sticky, not clammy like here.

I see Mr. Ramirez come out of his house, ready to clean the van. I watch him carry a bucket, rags, and a vacuum cleaner to the curb.

"Libby! Get away from that window." I turn away to see Ma scowling at me. Ever since the brick with the "stop" note was thrown at our house, she's afraid something might come hurtling through the window. She's getting herself ready to go clean houses, moving from kitchen to bedroom, straightening as she goes. She's changed from a nightgown to jeans and a T-shirt, and she grabs her keys and puts them in her mouth. She holds her jaw tight on the keys as she pulls her hair into a ponytail. When she's done with her hair, keys and purse in hand, she tells me to take out a package of hamburger around noon to thaw for dinner and to throw a load of clothes in the washing machine.

"Can you do that, Libby? I won't be able to get back home until late."

"God, Ma, what about Rita helping?" I should just be grateful she's not dragging me with her today.

Ma pushes her way out the back door butt first,

not saying anything more. The back door slams. I watch Ma walk toward the station wagon in the driveway. She gives Mr. Ramirez a critical glance before she gets in the car and backs it out and away.

Daddy gives all his attention to a yellow writing tablet. The knobs on his bent back show through his T-shirt the same way they did on the day he shined his shoes.

I pick up eggy plates and a wooden spoon crusted with food. I fill up the sink with soap and water and soak the dishes. I put the bacon grease from the frying pan into an empty orange juice container left on the counter. I'm taking care of business, just like Ma asked me to.

I go stand behind Daddy. His hair is slick with hair tonic. I wish he'd quit using it. Ma's been trying to talk him out of it too, telling him men don't use it anymore. We tell him he looks old-fashioned, like Elvis. I glance at his paper.

His handwriting is very precise. He would get good grades for his penmanship, even if he can't spell. Every vowel has a boxy shape, and he presses so hard on the paper, I would easily be able to read the marks on the page under it. That's the way it is with my daddy. Ma used to say that Daddy is a special person because of his way of seeing things. Loving someone like him isn't always easy, she says, but it's worth it in the long run. I wonder if she believes that anymore. She's working to get through the day. Never mind love. Never mind the long run.

I clean the dishes and grab a dish towel, and before long my hands are sopping wet from drying plates and glasses. I get another dish towel and place it flat on the table. I throw all the silverware on it and lightly run the towel over the forks and spoons and throw them into the silverware drawer. I'm hoping the rattle of the dishes will wake Rita, who's still in bed.

Daddy crumples up the paper he's been writing on.

He starts fiddling with the radio to get the perfect reception, the muscles in his jaw jumping. He gets the radio tuned to the Lake Michigan weather forecast. Three-foot waves today. Periods of light rain and fog. Small-craft advisory. Nearly every day is a small-craft advisory. Daddy loves listening to lake weather.

He waits for storms when the weather is good,

waits for calm if it's bad. Daddy can listen to Lake Michigan weather reports for hours, it seems. Wave reports, wind speed, whether or not you should sail. If he turns the radio off, he can barely sit still, afraid of missing something.

I went to the picket line once to see what Daddy does there. I took Angie with me. Daddy and the other men don't look anything like the wildcats I thought they were. They pace back and forth, mostly in silence, holding signs that say ON STRIKE or sitting on lawn chairs outside the shop. There are men they call scabs working in the shop who keep production going. That's what Daddy says Ma wants him to be. A scab. A strikebreaker. He acts tough, but his eyes are all about worry, that after all is said and done, he'll have no choice but to be one.

The strikers and scabs try to ignore each other, both wishing they were somewhere else. Outside the shop the strikers can smell engine oil, which Daddy says is a smell as good as home cooking for men who love parts and engines.

Mostly the strikers seemed tired and dull. Daddy says picketing is harder than it looks. The strike is a big chore. The strikers got sunburned right away because they weren't used to being out in the glaring sun all day. Cars go by and honk. The men anxiously wait for news from the union. They all hope for a favorable outcome so they can get back to work.

When me and Angie walked to the picket line, we got yelled at by Daddy in front of everybody; a picket line is no place for girls, he said. We protested but promised to go home. Then we snuck over to the sheet metal plant to prove to ourselves we couldn't be ordered around. They had the doors open, the ones that let the trains through, and we slunk past the guard to watch men who all looked the same, bathed in filth, welding things as big as walls. Guys taking a break invited us over, offered us white bread sandwiches glowing in their greasy palms. We thanked them and walked away.

Daddy turns off the radio and stands up. He's restless. On the way into the living room he kicks a pile of newspapers. The pages fly up the way seagulls do when you approach them at the beach. They go up slow and come down a little ways from where they started, ruffled. I follow Daddy into the living room. I'm glad he gets to feel what it's like being stuck at home.

The strike isn't going well. The union won't approve it, and all the guys out on the line are scared.

Daddy flops down on the couch and lights a cigarette. Tells me to get him an ashtray, and not the puny plastic one on top of the TV either. He tries to get comfortable, lying on the couch, wearing his running shoes. Daddy's favorite thing is to wear those track shoes. They feel just like slippers on his feet, he says. He wears them after he pulls the chips out of his work shoes. They are no-maintenance shoes, he says.

I locate the ashtray he wants and cross the room to get it.

It's heavy in my hand as I hand it to him. He sets it down on the coffee table he made and smiles at me. I pick up the newspapers still on the floor and stack them neatly on the coffee table. I'm restless too. The headline I read is something about the school board. I'm glad school is still weeks and weeks away.

Daddy turns his head and looks out the window. I look too. It's Mr. Ramirez, washing the Foxy Lady. He pulls out the floor mats, shakes them, and gets out the vacuum. The vacuum keeps asking why, why, why, and he works harder, getting at every crevice between the seats. Then he dips the rags into a bucket of soapy water. I'm sure it's warm water. Tenderly he soaps the Foxy Lady's face with the rags. I told Ma I hoped somebody would take such good care of me.

"No, you don't, Libby," she said. "Believe me." She said it as if the Foxy Lady van is evidence of some kind of mental problem.

One day not too long ago I got up the nerve to ask Mr. Ramirez about her. "Mr. Ramirez," I said, "is the Foxy Lady a good friend of yours?"

"Oh, yes," he said. He focused on gently wiping her face while I stood there. He didn't volunteer anything more.

"Did you paint her?" I asked.

"No. It's an art that only God gives some people."

I sat in the doorway of the van with the sliding door open, right on the Foxy Lady's shag carpet. It smelled like potato chips.

Mr. Ramirez spread his arms wide. "This van is like family, Leebee."

I nodded.

"Where I come from, to be able to drive something so beautiful to the park or even to the store is a big thing. Cleaning it is like going to church, getting holy sacrament," he said.

Toby would be surprised to know he and Mr. Ramirez believe the same thing about cars.

Daddy points his cigarette out toward the window at the van.

"Libby, let's get out of here." There's friendly ignition in his tone of voice. Some idea's percolating. My heart beats faster. He exhales, and we leave a cloudy living room behind us.

SINCE IT'S OVERCAST and a weekday morning at the beach, people are really spread out. A few animated kids are digging in the sand near the shore. No teenagers are at the snack bar. One lifeguard is on duty, and his face looks utterly blank as he stares into a nearly empty lake. He's probably the one who raked the dead alewives into clumps and picked up all the garbage. A mother grabs her child's arm to keep him from running into the lake, and he struggles and kicks at her. We inhale the tang of lake water and the stink of fish as we get closer to the water. I find a piece of driftwood that looks like the pommel of a saddle to give to Angie later. We sit down on the sand, and I shiver unconsciously. It's not cold, but the morning sun can't seem to punch through the clouds to provide any warmth. Coming here was a bad idea. Daddy taking a load off at the beach is not what Ma had in mind when she told me to take care of things.

Daddy pulls some change out of his shirt pocket. "You want anything, Libby?"

I tell him no. I can't let him spend any money.

"Daddy, are you sure we should be here?" I ask.

He puts his arm around my shoulder. "Don't worry," he says. My heart beats faster. Is he going to tell me we're moving again? I push my shoulders back and sit up straighter, shrugging off Daddy's touch. I need to be tough, to get ready. Maybe I should go get something at the concessions. I wish Angie were here. Or even Rita.

We sit side by side, neither one of us moving a muscle. Just inspecting the water. I think about Angie's question to me the day Kevin came home. What am I most afraid of? The answer seems to be changing.

The waves ripple widely, coming from the cold deep center, and crest with energy. The water grabbing the shore yanks so hard, a small ledge of sand has formed at the edge. The waves splash against it, and big, sloppy ripples reverberate back into the lake. The forward and backward waves crest and move together through the water like slippery fabric being zipped up. Small-craft-advisory waves.

Daddy sits with his back straight and his chin up. His hands, empty of a cigarette, rest on the sand. "Don't worry."

I nod and unclench my hands. My palms itch. I wonder how long we'll be here like this, how long we'll be anywhere. I know we should go home, but I'm drawn to watching the waves. Daddy's chest rises and falls as he submits his worries to the fishy Lake Michigan air and bows his head.

"You want to go in the water? I can teach you how to float."

I feel his question as if it were placed on the top of my head. I don't answer him. I think about the difference between Kevin and Daddy. Daddy would never bruise my arms or get mad over a haircut. One thoughtless clip of the scissors, and I am responsible for Angie's getting hurt. I have been pushing this thought away for days now, but the guilty feelings keep coming back.

Daddy doesn't beg or try to force me to learn to swim, as badly as I know he wants me to learn.

Daddy grips his forehead with one hand. The back of his hand has freckles and hair, and you can see the veins bulging all the way from his knuckles up the forearm. When I touch them, they are almost solid as muscle, and they move around under the skin. They've been that way almost his whole life. He said it's from carrying things that are too heavy.

Watching the backward retreat of each spent wave, I wish I had the power to go backward in time to the day I cut Angie's hair. I ask Daddy if he ever thought about time travel.

When we were little, Daddy would sometimes talk to us about his life growing up down south. He grew up in the country with no electricity or plumbing. They ate the same three things for every meal: pork, rice, beans. Packs of wild dogs roamed the ditches and threatened Daddy when he walked to and from school. He had to learn the hard way that farm animals are food. Men would get drunk on weekends and shoot at anything that moved, and women would stay inside with a Bible, praying. His stories always sounded far out and fearfully true.

He'd promised himself that we wouldn't ever experience such hardship.

He gestures me to come closer. "Have you ever heard of the Okefenokee Swamp?"

I say I have. Daddy knows I don't have the foggiest.

"Well, it's down in Georgia and a little ways in Florida. When I was a kid, we were in the Florida part for a little while after leaving Georgia."

"So?"

Daddy starts talking about the swamp: You can't see nothing down there at night, not even the hand in front of your eyes. There's things in the swamp that you can't tell what they are: boat people; spirits; pirates, maybe, who travel the murky waters; people who know every identical tree and the tiny differences between each drape of vine or moss. Daddy never met these mysterious people but knows for sure they exist.

Daddy had plans to find out once and for all what was in the swamp. They were big plans to go places. It took a few weeks to gather the wood, and he started to build a raft, stealing whatever rope or nails he could to put it together. Daddy had even sewn a flag together out of rags and a flour sack. Any proper pirate, high seas or not, needs a flag. He had a white flag too, just in case it would be smart to surrender. On the day it was ready, he told his brother that he was leaving for good and just wanted to say good-bye.

Daddy rubs his hands over the sand. He looks at me as if he's never seen me before. My hand goes to my throat. I feel invisible fingers touch the back of my neck; a tingle settles in my stomach.

Daddy's brother wanted to see the getaway raft. They joked all the way down the dirt road about it.

"He teased me about it, bad, until he saw it. Then he was actually impressed by my handicraft. When he set eyes on it, he said he wanted to ride it before I went off sailing the world with it.

"I said okay. I was proud. I thought he really liked it, you know? I guess he did. So I hopped on, and then he got on the raft too. It was a small raft; there wasn't a lot of room.

"We had a fight about that. He pushed me off and said he'd let me go when he got back. He was bigger, and he pinched my arm behind my back so I'd cry. Then he pushed that raft out into the swamp water and started floating away. I yelled at him to come back until I could barely see him. He was just going to go off with it, and I'd be stuck right there."

He stops talking and doesn't say any more, even when I say, "Daddy," over and over. Gulls complain. Waves smash into the shore. A jet flies over us, and we feel the rumble through our bodies.

AT ANGIE'S I knock on the door. Nobody answers even though I hear her music playing inside. I recognize the song from one of the CD's she's played for me. I knock louder and have a look in the door window to see if I can see anything at all. In the backyard nobody's at the picnic table. The roses on Char's rosebush have finished blooming and are all gone. A few dried and scraggly petals hang on. I pocket the driftwood I brought for Angie and grab the window ledge to her room and get up on tippy-toes to look in. That's when I see them.

Kevin is sitting on the edge of Angie's bed. His back is straight up, but his head is tipped back, as if he's looking for something on the ceiling.

Angie is kneeling before him on the zebra print rug, her head between his knees.

Kevin's fingers cover Angie's head like a catcher's mitt.

I hear him gasp over the music and sigh, the sound seeming to come right up through the floorboards, out the window, and into my chest.

Angie's hands look small and white, her red fingernails gripping his thighs, holding on.

He opens his eyes and sees me. He pushes Angie away from his lap so hard, her head hits the floor. Angie pulls herself up, and I see the front of her top is open. Then she sees me too. I close my eyes. When I open them again, I feel like I'm falling.

Chapter 11

After that, all I can think about is Angie. Angie and Kevin. I look around at this, our whole cruddy neighborhood; the best thing to do would be to leave.

The sidewalk outside the corner store is worn down from the trail of people who need something, any little thing—thread, a tomato, cigarettes, the owner's opinion. I push the door open and step over the threshold. As the store's screen door slaps behind me, I inhale deeply. The place smells like bologna and dust. I can't see a thing. My eyes have not adjusted from the brightness outside; the dimness makes me feel better. I head straight for the aisle with the soap and cleaning products. As I breathe in the comforting scent, I wonder what I should do.

The owner comes out from the back room with a few boxes and is at the counter unpacking bags of potato chips. He is wheezing. I keep a lookout through the shelving toward the counter.

I work hard at being invisible. If he saw me, he'd probably know that something was terribly wrong. How much trouble is Angie in? I tiptoe over to the only other aisle away from the counter.

Angie told me once that the women's hankies have been for sale forever. Nobody buys them. It's true. They've been here untouched since I moved here, one with a four-leaf clover embroidered on it, another with the letter M, and one with a red scalloped edge.

Did I even see anything, really? Kevin and Angie doing things with pants and shirts unbuttoned, things I was afraid to look at in those magazines. It plays in my head like an old-time silent movie, the one where the villain has tied the girl to the train tracks. I put my hands up to my temples to stop it.

I've never cared about the fancy hankies before,

but now I feel a powerful urge to have one. I check my pocket change to see how much I have. I'd love some Now-and-Laters but don't have enough for both. When I go to the counter with the red scalloped hankie, the owner looks at me funny but rings it up and takes my money. Angie called him a perfect pervert the day she took me to the tracks. I wonder if she had someone else in mind.

When I leave, I pull the handle and grab the door so it won't slam behind me.

As soon as I step over the groove in the pavement by the door, as soon as I know my heart won't quit on me, I walk fast.

AT THE TRACKS there are no trains. No sound of trains coming at all, not one sign of their passing. I wait. Wait some more.

I pull weeds away from the tracks. They sting my hands and turn them pale green. I smell the wild roses but don't pick them. They don't live past a minute off the bush. I go sit on the tracks and absorb the workings of Rubberville, everything smashed between clouds and sun. I try to think about other things happening on my block, besides what Kevin is doing to Angie. I would bet a car is pulling onto our street right now. The Foxy Lady is scorching away in front of my house, her smile dazzling God. Some kid is getting his hand slapped for reaching out to touch a hot stove. A jelly jar full of fresh-picked dandelions is wilting on a windowsill. I count out loud to a hundred and back down again. The wind roams through the rail corridor, keeping me from getting heat stroke.

I pick up a handful of stones and throw them one at a time at the tracks. I wish I had a penny I could put down on one of the rails so I could watch it be flattened.

The day Kevin and Angie showed me how to play pool replays in my brain. He explained when we were playing pool that if you sink the eight ball on the break, you've automatically lost the game. He said it was house rules. He joked with Angie about house rules.

I pull out the hankie and wave it overhead as if I'm a damsel in distress and need to be rescued. The noon lunch whistle blows in the distance. I realize I forgot to take out the hamburger and throw in the laundry. I let the hankie flutter from my hand to the ground.

● ● ●

THE BUSHES AT the tracks are sticking into my back, poking me, when Angie finds me. I force myself to say hi. Nothing more comes out, even after I open my mouth again. Dread rises in my throat. We watch the trains pass through like TV reruns. I scan the clacking cars, reading and counting: Santa Fe, Great Northern, Saskatchewan, Santa Fe, four, Santa Fe, five.

Angie speaks first. She tells me the Foxy Lady used to come here too, when she was around. "That's the legend anyway," says Angie.

"People come to the tracks to get sorted out, I guess," I say to Angie. She nods.

"A train. I can understand a train," I say. "There's not a lot to understand about a train."

Angie sits Indian style, cross-legged, with her eyes closed. She says, "Listen, listen to that." Trucks are driving down some street near the factories; the factories talk back. A kid's yell pops up from somewhere; a song from a radio flies out the window of a faraway car, speeding; the birds are going crazy; the wind is tossing things around down the tracks. Even though it still feels like summer, it seems as if a dusty rug has just been shaken out, choking the air.

Angie's hair is blown by the wind, and she keeps pulling strands of it out of her mouth. She tells me, "Nothing really happened between me and Kevin."

"Don't lie to me, Angie."

She lifts her chin. Picks at her fingernail polish; it's chipping off in spots. I take one of her hands and use my thumbnail to scrape some of it off. Angie says, "Ow, Libby," and pulls her hand away.

"It doesn't come off that easy," I say.

We rest together in the semishade of the bushes, flattening out the grass and brush.

I notice Angie's got new sandals on. I still have my same flip-flops, but I did get a new bra after her comment at the Sidewalk Sale Days.

Angie pokes my chest with her finger. "You know what? I think you're finally growing bigger titties now."

Her hand presses my chest. I feel like I'm on that amusement ride where the floor drops out. The area around the tracks where we've been sitting seems to whirl past when I shut my eyes. I open my eyes and look at the ragged red polish on Angie's fingernails jabbing my breastbone.

"That hurts," I say.

Angie sits up straighter and puts her arm around me. Her touch is warm. "Libby," she says. She pushes some sweaty hair off my forehead. I feel my lips turn down, but I won't cry. Angie touches my cheek.

We sit there, closely, in silence, neither of us moving. We are both holding our nail-bitten hands in our laps.

Angie says she thinks she might want Kevin.

"Do you mean, like a boyfriend?" I think about Angie and her stepdad together. "No way," I say.

"It's not like we're related." Silence slams into my chest.

"Have you guys done it?" I ask, shocked and also jealous.

Not all the way, she says, but they've done other things.

I think about the reproduction movie and the fashionable teacher who said it was important to use the right words. "With his penis?" I ask. Angie nods. He asked her to. He also touched other places. Somehow I knew it. I always sort of knew it. She tells me that some of the stuff he did with her felt good.

"He tells me I'm special."

I feel a hum come up through my body, a vibration from head to toe.

Before I came to Rubberville, I remember, we'd pass by towns on the highway, and Daddy would say about the small ones, "Blink and you'll miss it." Things in this world can be that small or that big. I don't blink at all when she tells me how it started.

She said it came about by accident. He'd come home tired from the duck farm and ask her for a back rub, and he'd give her one back. He told her he knew she had talent, that he could teach her how to play pool better. Whenever her hair fell in her eyes as she was setting up a shot, he'd brush it back. He started bringing her things like clothes and the paint-by-number sets. It was nice to have someone pay attention, to care so much about her.

"But what about the day I cut your hair? If he cares about you, why did he grab you so hard?"

She says he was just so upset. "He just loved my hair before, that's all," she says. Angie tells me he even cries sometimes because nobody understands him. His crying makes her feel sorry for him.

"There's something wrong with him, Angie. He's just . . ." I don't know the right words. "Do you really think it's okay to have your stepdad be your boyfriend? You should tell on him if he doesn't leave you alone," I tell Angie.

"Oh, please, get real, Libby." Angie is angry at me now.

"Aren't you afraid of him?" I ask. I sound pathetic and resentful, not at all convincing. I want to persuade her that something is wrong, really wrong. I want to jump up and holler at her. She seemed scared of him the day she didn't want me to leave, putting up a front of toughness but relying on me to be there. I was scared of him too. And then there were those bruises on her arm after the haircut.

I stare at Angie for something like an answer. She won't look me in the eye. I swallow hard and try to control the sour surge in my throat.

"Libby, just forget about it, okay? Please? Can you just do that for me because I'm asking? Because we're best friends?"

Usually when me and Angie sat together, even on day one, our arms or some body parts were touching, but now we sit apart from each other. Friends. I just don't know what that means anymore.

"You can't tell anyone," Angie says.

I pick up some rocks and start whipping them across the tracks. Despite my anger, they land softly in between the rails. Angie laughs. I cut her a look. It's not funny. She tells me I'm such a dork. A serious dork.

"Lighten up, Libby."

But I can't leave it alone. I try to make her promise to tell him to stop.

"Libby, I told you. Forget about it."

"I can't."

"You're making this into a big deal."

"Angie, Kevin's coming on to you is messed up, and you know it."

"That's what you think, Libby." Her voice is flat and cold.

She stands up and brushes grass and little pebbles off her butt. The rubble falls on my thighs. "I thought *you* were special too," Angie says. "I thought, of all people, you'd understand. I guess I just can't rely on anybody, huh?"

"C'mon, Angie. It's not that I don't care about what happens to you."

She turns on her heel. I jump up after her. "I can prove it. Don't go! Okay, I promise. I can keep a secret. Angie! I promise."

I sound hollow, as if I'm yelling into the tunnel under the tracks. I grab her hand in mine to make my pledge, and she shrugs me off and turns away. I watch her as she heads back to her house. It kills me to let her go in there alone, but I do.

Chapter 12

M a appears in our bedroom doorway, holding a palm-size plastic pink case in her hand. "You and I need to have a little talk."

I feel panic rise in my chest. She knows. She's going to want to know everything about Kevin and Angie.

I look to Rita and back to Ma.

Ma says, "I want to know what these are doing in this house."

She's waving the plastic pink compact case in the air with a dramatic flair she normally does not possess. I can't identify what it is she's got in her hand.

"A candy dispenser?" I say.

Ma throws it in the air. It lands next to me on my bed.

"Ortho-Novum." I read it out loud as if it's some code. Inside the little case are pills, numbers in a circle, and some of them have been punched out, eaten. The rising heat in my head cools.

"Birth control pills," Ma says. She's probably doing the same thing I am, adding up all the clues in Rita's latest mystery: the absences, harsh lipstick colors, syrupy perfumes, fewer complaints about the family.

I look at Rita, who gives me this look like, "Please, please don't tell on me." It's the same look Angie gave me just a few days ago. My heart skips. Now Rita's in some kind of trouble.

"Your father would be so disappointed."

Rita narrows her eyes at the mention of Daddy. Rita cuts Daddy no slack. He's out at the picket line, working hard not to give in to Ma's pleas for him to become a scab.

"Daddy, huh? What about you? Are you disappointed too? Like you should talk."

Rita's plainly disgusted, acting like she is not in

trouble but right about some hunch she's had. Ma crosses her arms at Rita's sulky face.

I don't move. I learned from wildlife shows that an animal stays still in order to become invisible. I want to hear this, not get kicked out. Ma stands firm in the doorway, her arms over her chest and her mouth a straight line.

Rita goes on. "At least I'm not stupid enough to turn out like *you*, have kids before you barely turn twenty, marry the first sap who comes along because you have to and be stuck. What I'm doing is *different*." Rita says it like it is three words. "Diff-er-ent."

The truth sits there on my bed: a neat circle of pills.

"Who is it? Who is the boy?" Ma is one hundred percent snide.

"Frankie Bonar."

"What? Does Angie know?" I ask.

Ma and Rita look at me. "Does she?" Rita nods her head. Angie has struck me down again.

"Listen here, Miss Mature, you are in way over your head," Ma says. "You have one choice here. Go by the rules of this house. You're not to see *that* boy. You're grounded." I wonder if her mother said that to her about Daddy.

In the silence that follows Ma's ruling, Ma turns away from Rita and storms out.

I'm still absorbing the news that Angie knew about Rita's love affair with Frankie, and that Ma was pregnant before she and Daddy got married, when Rita throws herself on the lower bunk.

I can't believe my sister went all the way. With Frankie. And Angie knew. She held out on me. I think about Rita and Frankie doing what I saw Angie and Kevin doing, and I can't stand it.

"She doesn't want me to see Frankie anymore, but I love him! I don't care what anybody says. I don't care." Rita starts bawling like she's being strangled.

"So how did she find them?" I pick up the pill pack on my bed and examine it. The pills look too tiny to do all they are supposed to. I ask Rita to quit crying and tell me what happened.

"I forgot and left them on the bathroom sink."

"Why Frankie?" Without me knowing. Me. I'm the one who shares this room with her, the one who listens to her thousand complaints.

I lie there. Betrayed.

My sister heaves heavy sobs in the bunk under mine. She says Frankie says the most wonderful things. He adores her. There is no keeping them apart. His kisses make her feel alive. She doesn't care about us, her stupid family, our crazy parents, this house we live in. She just wants to get out of here and be with him.

Suddenly I'm in a rage.

"You lying little sneak," I say to her, not sure if I'm talking to her or to Angie.

"I hate you," she says.

The next day Rita tells me again how much she hates me for everything: the fact that I called her a lying sneak, that I think Frankie is a jerk, that basically I don't know anything about love. I am not to borrow a single thing from her ever again.

"Not one thing. You got that, twerp?" she says. Plus she'll never speak to me again. She acts as if it's my fault she's grounded for doing it with Frankie.

Rita now spends her time looking up at the ceiling, moaning over Frankie. I'm sorry she fell for him. She breaks down when I ask her again why Frankie and not someone smarter or nicer.

Rita paces back and forth in our bedroom,

explaining to me how Frankie is perfect. She even shows me how he likes to kiss her, with a hand on my shoulder, the other hand placed at the back of my tilted head. She likes running her hand through his hair, looking into his eyes. His lips are smooth. She stops short of actually kissing me, but the waxy smell of her lipstick up close curdles my gut.

She talks about the last time they were together as if Frankie had died and gone to heaven. "You can't stop destiny," Rita says. The life they will have together is going to be better than anything they've ever known. I wonder if Ma felt that way about Daddy. She must have.

Rita says she didn't want to go to her grave a virgin. I'm pretty sure I will, and I'm not sure how I feel about that yet.

After a while Rita asks me something. "Libby, if you were on your deathbed right now, what would you be most proud of in your life?"

"God, Rita. I'm not answering a corny question like that." But I answer in my head. I won't be on my deathbed till I've saved Angie from Kevin and we're true friends forever—a cornball answer to her cornball question. "You tell *me*, since you're acting like you're on your deathbed."

"I just think . . . um, I just think that there's so much we can do. I mean, Libby, why are we on this planet? I mean, what *are* we here for? It seems we are here to figure out the world's problems. I'd like to do that. To fix them. Like Daddy's trying to do."

I had no idea. I thought while Rita was lying around, she wasn't thinking about anything.

"There's so much hate and cruelty and sadness and starvation. In social studies last year we saw these pictures of people in Africa who were like walking sticks with basketball-size stomachs. I almost threw up in class. Mr. Jezak gave me a pass." She hugs her arms to herself.

I want to shake Rita. She thinks all the screwed-up things in the world are happening somewhere else. But bad things are happening right here. Where people like us live.

"But there's something you can do around here," I say.

"Like what?"

Again, I consider asking her for advice about Angie. Rita's eyes are rimmed red, swollen, defiant. She'd rather move to Zimbabwe than try to fix anything that's wrong in Rubberville.

"You could sneak out and buy me a Dilly Bar at the DQ."

I WAKE UP in the night, and my whole body is shaking.

"Rita?" I whisper down to her bunk. Her breathing is deep and regular. Even though I don't want to move, I climb down to go to my sister. My knees wobble when my feet hit the floor.

I touch Rita's shoulder. Whenever I was scared as a kid, Rita would wrap me up with her in her big-girl blanket and protect me. I hope she's too sleepy to recall all my snotty comments about Frankie or remember that she hates me.

I stand next to her bunk, behaving like a ghost waiting to spook somebody. She eventually moves.

When she finally sees me standing next to her bed, she sits up, concerned. "Libby? Is it the panther?" I used to have a recurring nightmare about a stalking panther. This time I dreamed about Kevin.

"Yes," I say, shivering in my gown even though it's still pretty warm in here. I've never been so scared for myself or Angie.

She moves over and fluffs her sheet over me, just the way she used to when I was little. She used to like taking care of me. I used to think Rita had superpowers.

In my dream Kevin had a knife in one hand and the driftwood I picked up at the beach for Angie in the other. He was grinning. "We're going to play a Will You Tell? game," he said, and he made me stand up against a wall. He put his face close to mine and stood before me with an uneven smile. In the dream I wanted to run away, but not one of my muscles would move. Kevin put the piece of driftwood on top of my head. He then put his free hand under my chin. I couldn't squirm or move. "Libby, answer me," he said.

His hands gripped my jaw hard, and he said he was going to knock that piece of shit off my head. He laughed and said he wasn't going to let any girl ruin his life. He walked back a few paces and raised his arms and started to count. "One . . . two . . . three." I pushed out against the wall with all my strength, and felt blood rush through my arms and breath fill my lungs again. That's when I woke up.

I settle in next to my sister, the warm sheet over

my chest, and feel another wave of panic come through me. I wonder what Kevin would do if I told anyone.

ALL THROUGH THIS week the strike has been a disaster. The strikers have been given donations to help with expenses, but it's not nearly enough. Ma's been working a lot to make up for it. Everyone has to help. Toby's been trying to make up the difference with his body-shop earnings. I've been helping Ma vacuum and dust on housecleaning jobs. Even Rita has been helping keep house and cook dinner. She's trying to get back in Ma's good graces so she can start seeing Frankie again.

During Ma and Daddy's last fight about the strike, Daddy kept saying there was a line that shouldn't be crossed. "It's a matter of standing together," he said. If he went back to work, where would that leave the other guys? Ma said she didn't care about the other guys. "Why don't you stand up for us, go back on the production line and bring in a paycheck? School starts soon, and the kids have nothing. Nothing!"

Daddy claimed he *was* standing up for us. He was

making a statement about the importance of sticking together: If people don't watch out for each other, how can they look at themselves in the mirror every morning?

Everything Daddy says makes sense to me. I keep Angie's secret because she asked me to. I understand I would be a traitor otherwise. No better than a scab.

MA BACKS OUT of the long driveway away from the house we just cleaned. She drives two more blocks and then pulls over to the side of the road. We park in front of a house with a perfect lawn and a half-moon driveway. A tree shades the road over us, but it's still beastly hot. She lifts herself up away from the steering wheel and twists and leans over toward the floor of the backseat. She pulls up the paper grocery bag she was looking for.

It's our lunch. Slices of white bread, Velveeta cheese, and a bunch of purple grapes. "I like to eat around here if I can," Ma says. "This place looks like a park, don't you think?" I take a bite of my sandwich, and immediately the bread and cheese stick to the roof of my mouth and the sides of my teeth. I hate that feeling, but I love Velveeta. I ask Ma if she brought any extra slices, and she says yes. When I finish my sandwich, I unwrap a single cheese slice and place a piece of it in my mouth.

All day I've been thinking about Angie. As I ran the vacuum back and forth over the wall-to-wall carpet, I thought about Angie, kneeling on the zebra skin rug. All morning I tried to push those thoughts aside. I tried not to cry. I know telling might be the equivalent of being a scab, but maybe not. Maybe I'm missing the point. Kevin is taking advantage of Angie. I know at least one person who would agree with me: Ma.

I open my eyes and look out the window, away from my mother's chapped hands on the wheel and her flyaway hair. I want her to explain our life. Why Rubberville?

"Libby, what is it?" asks Ma. "You've been awfully quiet lately."

I feel the static in my chest I'm hoping to clear. Our car is hot from the vinyl seats and, now that our lunch is gone, smells faintly of pine cleaning solution and Velveeta.

"You promised if I ever wanted to talk about"— I decide to be specific—"sexual intercourse—"

"Sexual intercourse? Libby, why on earth? What

did Rita tell you?" Then she checks herself. She did promise.

I tell Ma that Rita got me curious because of her trouble with Frankie. But it's not Rita. What's bothering me are things I cannot put into words. Angie. The idea that she could be in love with her stepdad. Or something worse. Our friendship doesn't seem to mean anything to Angie. She has chosen Kevin over me. She wants to pretend nothing ever happened.

"Ma, I want to know what is so great about sex."

Ma looks ready to hyperventilate, but she steadies herself and puts her hand under my chin to look me in the eye. Her hand is warm. I'd like to push my chin into her chest, cry about everything that's wrong, but I hold myself up. I'm too proud for that.

Ma pushes some stray hair lock back behind my ear before she speaks. Her tenderness makes me feel ashamed of myself. I look down at my hands. They are almost as bad as hers.

She says, "I have always wanted you girls to be happy. I have my doubts about Frankie, but your sister has a good head on her shoulders." She really thinks that about Rita? Now it's my turn to be shocked.

"Someday someone will realize how special

you are," Ma says.

"But, Ma, what about . . ." I move my hand in a gesture toward my lap. Ma's thighs look flattened and pudgy on the seat next to me. I look at the space between her legs in her shorts and have a hard time imagining kids could have come out of there.

"Oh." I think she hoped she'd answered my question already. "When you're in love, it's a wonderful feeling."

"I heard it hurts." Rita just about said as much, even though she acted like it was so great and worth all the trouble.

"Well it takes a little getting used to," Ma admits. I can tell she doesn't want me to be too interested or scared.

"What if you don't want to?"

"Libby, what's this about?"

I look out the windshield at the road and tell her I don't know.

"I have to be honest with you, Libby—I've been concerned about what's been going on with you girls this summer—Rita, now you, even Angie. It seems like you're all growing up too fast."

"What if you really love someone?" I think about

that first time in Angie's room, the day I heard that "I'm in You" song. A car drives by us at a good clip and seems to suck air out of the car. The rubbery smell of asphalt rises from the road in the car's wake. I'm with my mother, but I've never felt so alone.

"It's hard to say if what Rita is feeling right now is love," Ma says.

"Oh." Who cares about Rita? Of course she's not in love.

"And that Angie. That girl is just headed for big-time trouble." I search my mother's face with renewed interest for what Ma seems to understand about Angie.

"Ma, she's my best friend." Used to be my best friend.

"That may be so, but there are other girls in the world. In a few weeks you'll be starting high school." The thought of school makes my forehead burn.

"As if we're going to stick around long enough for me to make new friends," I say with all the force-fulness I can muster. Every time things get hard to handle, we move away.

I think about boring old Doris. That's the kind of friend my mother wants for me. I press my fingers into the door handle. I should just open it and walk away.

Ma reaches over to reassure me, strokes my arm. Her hand feels rough on my skin. Tears suddenly roll out the sides of my eyes. I dig my fingernails into the seat cushion.

"Hey, Libby. I just don't want you to start getting into trouble, that's all." I feel the bread and cheese inching its way back up my throat.

I think about the stuff I've done she doesn't know about—the beer drinking, the magazines, almost stripping—and I think, Maybe she's right; I'm growing up too fast. But I'm not the one in trouble.

Chapter 13

I promised Angie I'd try to forget. But I can't. Angie hasn't spoken to me since we argued at the tracks. I go over to her house and knock on the door even though I'm worried Kevin might be there. Nobody answers. I grab the window ledge to Angie's room and get up on tippy-toes to look in. My heart beats faster, wondering what I'll see in there this time. Nobody. Peeling paint on the window ledge is rubbing my palms raw. Inside, things look undisturbed. Nothing going on. Her bed is made, as usual.

I take a seat at the picnic table and wait. I'm relieved nobody's home. It gives me time to think.

I'm also worried about what to say to Angie.

I think about Kevin's face, the look in his eyes when he saw me looking into Angie's bedroom. And then?

I put my hands on the table and rest my head in my arms. I breathe into the crook of my elbow. I wish I could be anywhere but here. I'm trying hard not to cry by breathing steadily toward the ground. The grass under the picnic table is longer than in the rest of the yard, and I push my feet through the tall, resistant blades.

I look up when I hear tinny music. Char's car comes into view in the driveway. She's got the windows down, and the radio is on really loud. I sit stock-still and hold my breath. When she kills the engine in the driveway in front of me, the car gives a little gurgle and a cough. Then silence.

Char reaches over to the passenger side and rolls up the window. Her head bobs in awkward time as she starts singing the song that was playing on the radio before she turned off the car. Some song about thunder when it rains and the players who love you only when they're playing. She doesn't see me sitting at the picnic table, watching her jerky movements and hearing her cracking voice. She's really a terrible singer.

She turns and grabs something out of the backseat and opens the car door. Char tosses her hair and adjusts her sunglasses. As she closes the car door, she finally becomes aware of me sitting at her picnic table and pulls her shopping bag close to her chest.

"Libby. Jesus Christ. You scared the shit out of me." She adjusts her sunglasses again.

"Hi, Char." I squint at her.

The bag in her hand is bulging with frozen dinners. It looks as if she got one of every kind.

"Where's Angie?" she asks.

"I don't know. I've been waiting for her," I say.

Char asks me do I want something while I wait, Coca-Cola or some chips or something? I get up to go. It was a dumb idea to come over.

Char insists I stay.

She goes inside and soon comes back with a drink for herself and a bottle of soda and a bag of Fritos for me. I go straight for the Fritos and eat as if I have not eaten for days.

Char says, "So how come you're here without Angie? I thought you two girls were tight."

She takes a sip of her drink. I notice there's a greenish-yellow tint around the edge of her left eye; she's hiding it behind the sunglasses.

I shrug; thinking about Angie brings back the lump in my throat.

I want to tell her I saw Angie on the floor in her bedroom, kneeling on the zebra print rug. Kevin's hands were on top of Angie's head, her face pushed into his lap. His fingers covered Angie's head like a catcher's mitt. These things rest on the tip of my tongue. With every single Fritos, I push the words down. I can't get a sound out.

Char smells like vanilla perfume; I wonder if she suspects anything at all about what's happening with Angie and Kevin.

"You hear that?" Char asks.

"Hear what?" I say.

Char cocks her head; her hair falls past her neck in a hank. "That?"

"Char, I don't hear anything." Not even the ice in her glass moves.

"That's right. You don't. Peace and quiet for once. They say you always love your kids, and I guess I do, but today's one of those days when—"

I think about the day at the tracks when Angie said to me, "Listen, listen to that," and we heard the workings of Rubberville going on around us. It bothers me how much Angie can be like her mother.

Char grabs a handful of chips out of the bag, which I hold still for her. She tosses her head back and throws the chips in her mouth and gulps down her drink. She has a tattoo of a rose on her left arm, and it moves with her muscle. She doesn't seem the type for motherhood.

She drains her glass, and she's squinting now, cat-like. I wonder what she used to look like before she had all her problems with men. When she was my age.

I look down at the picnic table. The angles on everything seem off. It must be the heat. I look up at the puffy clouds in the sky to clear my head a little.

Char finishes her drink and is chomping on an ice cube. Distracted. I feel frozen in space. It has taken every nerve I have to come over here, but I realize there is no way Angie will ever listen to me.

I stand up and say, "Nice talking with you, Char." Finally I know exactly what I have to do.

• • •

I STEP INTO our kitchen. "Ma, I need to talk to you about Angie," I say.

I pull out a chair and sit as if I won't have the strength to get back up. I watch Ma get a pot of coffee going. She slides a can of coffee across the countertop toward the coffeemaker. She pulls the lid off the can and takes a whiff. She turns to me and says, "I love the smell of coffee in the can." I say, "Me too." Then she counts out four scoops and puts each one into the basket at the top of the coffeemaker. When she's done, Ma leans back against the countertop with her arms crossed, and looks at me.

"What's the matter, Libby?" Her eyes bore into mine.

I think about the big scratch I put in the floor at one of the cleaning jobs with Ma. She moved a rug over it, and we kept quiet about it. We should have told someone, but we were too tired and scared by the time we finished the job. We drove home in silence, each of us feeling guilty. I didn't want Ma to lose work because of my clumsiness. The strike has made it so we're getting even farther behind on bills. Ma's trying not to rely on me, but she needs my help more than ever. Now that I understand I shouldn't be helping her so much, I want to. Over at Angie's, family doesn't seem to matter one iota.

"I don't know how to explain it."

"Uh-huh." Ma nods and doesn't say anything more, ready to listen.

How do I talk about the time Angie nearly pushed me onto the tracks when a train was coming but that she held me tight, as if I were the whole world? Do I describe how she protected me from Danny at the pony rides but then gave in to her mother, forcing me to join her? How we both were freaked out by Kevin's knife routine and his sick magazines with the girls in them but that Angie still plays pool with him, and who knows what else? How Angie stripped in front of me once and now acts as if we never met. My throat hurts. How do I begin?

The smell of fresh coffee is heartening. Ma gets two clean mugs out of the dish rack by the sink, fills them, and sets one cup down by me at the table.

Then Ma takes a seat and, holding on to her mug, blows on it and takes a sip. "I want you to try it this way before your father ruins it for you with all that sugar." Daddy loves milk and three scoops of sugar in his coffee. He always jokes he could live on a pot of coffee and half a pound of sugar a day. With the strike dragging on, he might have to.

I blow on the mug real hard and take a big sip. It's terrible. Bitter. It burns my throat, and tears come to my eyes.

Ma's hair falls in one eye as she looks down at me, sleuthing me out. My head is spinning. I feel I could pass out. I try to pick up the coffee mug, but my hand shakes. I'm afraid I'll spill, so I put the cup back down. I bend my head toward the cup and put my lips to the coffee mug and slurp.

Ma ignores my table manners. The lump in my throat grows. After Angie made me promise not to tell, she's cut me out.

I remember Angie's head hitting the floor, hard, when Kevin saw me watching and pushed her away. When she pulled herself up, I saw the front of Angie's top was open.

"Kevin likes to play pool with Angie. He says she's the next Minnesota Fats."

"Uh-huh. And does Angie like to play pool with Kevin?" The question stabs me.

"Kevin's acting like he's in love with Angie, and

she thinks she is too."

"What do you mean, Libby? Does Angie have a crush on Kevin?"

"Yes and no," I reply.

"Oh?"

"It's really weird, Ma. He touches her private places. She touches his."

"What?" My mother sits up straighter. I sense something inside her has cracked open. It is as if all our troubles because of the strike don't matter.

She asks me if I've ever seen anything strange, any unusual behavior.

Everything I've seen is unusual and strange. "I saw it," I say.

So I tell Ma. I tell her everything. Everything.

Ma listens and doesn't shift in her seat. At first her eyebrows go up, then relax as if she's weary. Her brows knit together.

"Kevin's actions are criminal," she says when I'm done talking. "He's stepped over a boundary with Angie," she says. Ma stands up and grabs a phone book.

I feel myself go numb. "Ma? What are you doing? Is Angie going to get in trouble?"

"No, honey," she says. "Kevin's the one who crossed the line, not Angie."

Ma reassures me that it was good I told, that something needs to be done. Telling her about Angie and what I saw is a starting point. Telling Angie's secret is the very thing Ma says will help Angie. Nothing to be afraid of, not even Kevin. I did nothing to be ashamed of.

I watch her page through the phone book, watch her fingers nimbly dial, and feel my heart rate rise. As the relief of sharing this secret with my mother spends itself, I start to feel angry. To me it always felt that Ma was against Angie, that she didn't want me to be friends with her.

I am consumed with regret. No more lying on Angie's bed talking, no more listening to the "I'm in You" song. As long as I live, I'll never know anyone like Angie.

I sit at the table feeling every inch the two-faced tattletale. I have never done anything, good or bad, that comes with so many repercussions. I stare at the yellow and gold linoleum squares on the kitchen floor, trying to make sense of the pattern. I listen to Ma repeat word for word all that I said. Her voice shakes. I follow the dirt in the cracks and feel annoyed that the design doesn't exactly match, while Ma tells someone at child protection the whole thing.

I think about what Ma said, that this is a starting point. To me it feels like the end.

Chapter 14

It doesn't take long before Angie finds out I told. One whole day, to be exact. She stands out on the sidewalk in front of my house and demands I come out. I keep my head up as I open the screen door and step out of the house. She could do anything to me: punch me, kick me, pull my hair. I stiffen up to get ready, but I won't stop her. I can't blame her for wanting to kill me.

"Guess what, Libby," she says as I stand before her, ready for judgment. Her eyes are puffy from crying, and her arms are stiff at her sides. Her clothes are wrinkled, as if she's slept in them. Angie's voice rises. For someone who didn't want anyone to know anything before, she's willing to make a big scene right on the street.

"Some lady from social services called yesterday." Her teeth are clenched. Her voice is cold and ragged. I feel turned to stone.

"Char had to take me downtown and give a statement. Like, this lady wanted to know if I've ever seen Kevin *naked*. And what specifically happened on the afternoon of August third." She lifts her head, staring into my face, her voice stinging my ears.

"It was you, Libby." She pushes me, and my shoulders draw back automatically. "Admit it, you big fat coward." What I did took a lot more courage than she'll ever know. Her breathing is coming in bursts, and her face is really red.

I remember when Angie was kneeling on the zebra print rug and I heard Kevin breathe deeply and sigh. The thought passes through my chest, nauseating me.

"And then that lady served Char some papers and said Kevin is ordered out of the house while an investigation is pending." Angie's hands stretch her rumpled T-shirt. Her shorts look heavy on her body, as if there's sand weighing down every pocket.

"Mom's been fucked up ever since, and she totally blames me. Libby, Kevin's probably going to go to jail."

Goose bumps automatically rise up on my arms. I look out at the street we're on.

Angie kicks at an anthill that's been building in the cracks between sidewalk slabs. One swipe and she's destroyed their whole little world, just as I've done to hers. I touch the anthill sand with my foot. I wish Angie had never come over that day she took me to the tracks, that she had stuck to her side of the street. Then I wouldn't have had any secrets to tell or not to tell. Nobody would be going to jail on my account. The frightening power of sending someone to prison wells up in me.

"Angie . . . I had to." I need to explain it to her. My world is entirely blown apart too, and I'm paying for it with loneliness and a broken heart.

I consider blaming Ma, saying she had her suspicions and dragged it out of me. That might make Angie understand and eventually forgive me. I don't think Ma would even mind if I said that, but I can't lie to Angie. My palms sweat, and I rub them on my thighs. "You know. It just seemed . . . wrong."

Angie breathes in deep when she hears that word. Wrong.

"I got to thinking, Angie. If a guy says he loves you, he's not going to hide it from anyone. If you have a dad or stepdad, he's especially not supposed to do or say anything to, like, get you to do sexual things with him." What Kevin was doing wasn't love. It was spoiling the idea of love.

"You're my *friend*, Angie. That means something to me. You mean something to me. I couldn't let that keep happening to you."

I thought about the time me and Rita made our cat go crazy. It felt so good to be cruel; we couldn't stop ourselves. We shoved it in a bookcase that had these sliding doors. We'd open one door behind it, and it would try to run out, and then we'd open the other door and shut it quick again. It ran back and forth, no way out. Our hands were a blur to the cat, Rita's fingers and then mine in its face. We finally let it out when it started meowing, weirdly and deeply insane. It ran away, and we never told anyone why.

My feet feel rooted in place as I stand out here with Angie.

I remember Daddy saying, the night all the men

169

from the shop came over, that there are certain reasons people do things. That sometimes the reasons can be really personal. Can't she see that I care about her so much that I'm willing to sacrifice our friendship over it?

I start over.

"Angie, you're someone I care about so much that I—" That's all I can say. Pathetic. I didn't know I could ever feel so numb, emptiness pushing against my heart.

"I thought you were my friend." Angie's voice is an accusing whisper devoured by all she has been holding against me. "I hate you, Libby."

She punches me in the stomach. I feel all the air rush out of me at once, and I double over. It hurts so bad. I hear her feet slap the pavement righteously step by step as she walks away.

I hold my side where she hit me and feel the rise and fall of my breath in my hands. I feel dizzy, but I hold my ground.

AFTER I COULD stand upright again, I started walking. Spent my day wandering the streets of Rubberville and beyond. I've been thinking about how I passed the do-the-right-thing test but flunked out with Angie. I'm not a philosopher, but it seems that if you stand up for something you believe in, there are always consequences, even if you don't get socked in the stomach.

When this summer started, I was hoping to make friends. I didn't set out to change the course of anyone's life—hers, mine, or Kevin's. I spoke up. And that's still a shock to me.

Dusk is coming on strong now. A motion detector light goes on at the nearest house, and I get a better view of things. I look behind me toward the garbage cans on the side of the house. I tell myself it was a dog, nothing worse, that tripped the lights. Nobody whose name starts with the letter K. I can smell whatever it is the neighbors had for dinner tonight, and the night before that, and the night before that. Must be fish sticks and Tater Tots.

The streetlights go on from up on the little hill. The telephone poles look like a clean line of crosses in the dusk. I should probably go home.

A set of car headlights punches my pupils. As the car gets closer, I recognize Toby. I wave at my brother, driving up in the family car.

"Hey, there you are," says Toby over the car engine's drone. "Have you been out here all day? Ma sent me looking for you."

I shrug. I get in the car on the passenger side.

When Toby pulls away, he says, "Libby. Jesus Christ."

"What?"

"Ma told me about you telling on Angie's step-dad." He runs his hand through his hair. "That's some crazy shit, Libby," he says.

"What would you have done?" I ask him.

"I don't know. Kick Kevin's ass maybe. I don't know."

We drive past Daddy's factory and watch two men feed a fire in a metal barrel. At night only two of them sit out there at a time. Everybody does his fair share of picketing, but the number of guys out at the same time, day or night, has dwindled.

When my brother gets the chance, I know he drives around alone in the wagon and sings along to music in the car. He doesn't have any real friends in Rubberville. It's all Springsteen.

We recognize one of the guys on the line, and Toby honks at him. It's Carl Nelson. He runs up to the car. "Hey, boy," he says to my brother.

"Fuckin' A," says Toby. Carl reaches in the car, and they give each other some brotherhood hand-shake.

Toby says, "Hey, check this out: I've got a song about working in a factory." He fiddles with the stereo in the car. "Something I wrote." I gain new respect for my brother. He's not only lip-synching but writing his own songs these days. Carl looks ready to bolt. Before Toby gets it cued, Carl goes, "Hey, bro, I got to get back on the line, but maybe some other time. If this song is about going on strike, I'd like to hear the whole thing sometime."

Carl plops down in a lawn chair and picks up his picket sign. He acts as if it weighs a hundred pounds and smiles at us. Toby gives Carl the peace sign.

My brother pulls away from the curb and hits eject on the player. I really wanted to hear it.

"Hey, Toby, put it back in. C'mon."

Instead, Toby says we should just blow out of town, never come back, get away from all the small-minded crap that keeps a person down.

My brother puts in Springsteen again. He belts out the lyrics along with him. Toby says Springsteen's music is about the bigger picture, the lie of the American Dream. "A person with that idea has some other concept besides living and dying in some dumb-shit town," Toby says.

I want to tell Toby Angie punched me, but I just shift in my seat and agree with him. With all my heart.

He says, "That's it, Libby. We're outa here." I feel like he read my mind.

Toby hits eighty mph as soon as we pass a street-light on the main drag heading out of town. Soon he has the car cranked up to eighty-five, ninety, every-thing blurry on the street. The whine of wind through the window seals accelerates my fear. We keep going. The houses get larger, more modern, each and every one with aluminum siding and a big picture window with pressed drapes, a driveway, bushes trimmed in perfect circles and rectangles.

Suddenly he stops the car. My head almost hits the dash.

"Sometimes people go crazy." He says it like it is one of the Ten Commandments. I nod. I'm caught in a crossfire I don't understand.

We take Highway 11 straight west.

"Let's go all the way to the Pacific Ocean," I tell Toby. I want to go somewhere much bigger and more vast, somewhere I could swim with the dolphins if I wanted to.

After about an hour we leave all traces of the city behind. We have gone past places Daddy has never taken us, and I sit on my hands. I'm starting to feel like a serious runaway. I'm suddenly alert. My palms sweat underneath my thighs. The towns we pass through are dinky and falling apart. The people who live in them will have nothing their whole lives.

My brother tells me pretty soon this whole state is going to be one big cornfield owned by one big company. Bruce is defiantly against all that. I wonder if Bruce is also against what happened to Angie.

Miles later we get to this point where the hills get much bigger, and the farmhouses are settled into deep valleys; their utility lights are bright pinpricks in the dark element of earth. The houses dip in and out of view as we ride up and down the swells of the hills. How many of these houses have people who turn girls into sad liars because there's no other way they can live with what happens to them?

My stomach has a hard time keeping pace, and I

swallow hard to keep from throwing up.

I tell Toby I'm feeling a little barfy. He says to look at the steady line at the side of the road, not the broken center line. We quit talking because I have to train my eyes to look up past the edge of the car hood to the side of the undulating road.

The car doesn't break down; it runs out of gas. Compared with the hum of the engine and the wind whining in the cracks of the window seals, it now sounds deathly quiet on this road with nothing but the moon shining on the cornfields all around us. The stalks of corn chafe in a slight breeze, a papery, lonely sound. We get out of the car and hear the weight of the car doors slam. We both breathe deeply, inhaling the smell of dust and clover and cow shit and whatever else is out here. I feel my stomach expand, bloated and full as if I'd eaten a huge bowl of oatmeal. We did it. We blazed out of Rubberville.

Toby is wearing a bandana, the boots, the jeans, but he's less like Springsteen, more like himself. We don't say a word to each other.

My brother takes off his bandana and wipes his forehead. We walk into the dark cornfield. Nobody knows where we are except the ripening cobs, tightly closed. We walk against the direction of the rows of corn, knocking away stalks. The air carries the sounds of passing cars on the highway and whispering corn tassels. We go faster, straight down the rows, then switch and struggle onto the path of the cornstalks again. I try not to trip on the fingery roots of corn and knobs of soil in the field. The sky is far above, ripped up by corn tassels. We do this until we are doubled over. Then we lie side by side, in a row, gasping.

WE WALK FOR what seems like miles along the edge of the highway. I pick up a handful of gravel and drop pieces as I suppose Hansel and Gretel did, hoping to find their way back. My brother's boots scuff the gravel, and my flip-flops slap at my heels. They should have disintegrated a while ago, but they haven't yet. That's the miracle I'm settling for right now. The gas station we find is at the border. Iowa. I tell my brother we'll find what we're looking for in Iowa, somewhere nobody knows our history. My brother tells me to cut the shit. We're getting gas, and we're going back. Home. That's what he called it. Home.

The gas station guy looks at us squinting at him

from under the bright fluorescent lighting as if he's never seen sorrier-looking people in his life.

He offers to call our folks. Toby turns him down, says we don't live too far from here, but takes the ride the guy offers to get us back to our car. After we get going again, Toby asks me if I've got some money and looks worried when I shake my head no. He didn't think about gas or money when we left. At the time it seemed we would just fly away into the blur. I'm certain Ma and Daddy are seriously worried about where we are, and I feel a thick band of doubt settle on my head. My brother starts playing Springsteen's music again but doesn't sing along. I train myself not to get carsick, not to think about what we're going back to.

We get to the edge of Rubberville, and the car conks out again. Again we start walking, my shoes flapping and his scuffing.

"Leebee!"

I look up from the side of the road and see the Foxy Lady van and Mr. Ramirez. I'm so happy to see him that I jump in front of the van toward the driver's side window, ready to throw my arms around him.

Some tinny Latin music wafts out from inside the

van. It's nothing at all like the deep, hollering tones of the singer I've been hearing all night, and it is a relief. A carnival in comparison with Springsteen. Mr. Ramirez opens the door for me and beckons my brother into the van with his free arm. Finally I get to ride in the Foxy Lady van. As I sit down on the passenger seat, my feet feel like blocks, swollen and sore between my toes from walking. Heat like hot breath radiates from inside the van. I inhale the Foxy Lady smell, potato chips, and realize I'm starving.

Toby is still standing at the roadside, hands in his pockets. His T-shirt is rumpled, and his jeans look dirty. I half expect him to decline the ride, but then he pulls open the sliding door and slouches into the van. He sits down on the orange shag in back and runs his fingers over the carpet.

Mr. Ramirez pulls away from the curb, giving us a ride home.

I ask him about the Foxy Lady again, if she was a real person.

"Oh, my angel, of course! *Dios mío*," he says, and looks up.

"How come you say that?"

"She was only trying to make a better life. Like so

many." Mr. Ramirez pulls his chin into his chest and takes a deep breath. I hope he doesn't cry. I couldn't handle that.

"You mean she's dead?" I ask.

"No. *Gone*," he says. "She wanted things."

"Like what things?" I ask.

"Freedom," he says. I expected him to say she wanted something expensive, a better house or car, or a fairy-tale ending.

"Is that why you put her face on your van?"

Mr. Ramirez nods. "To always remember. There is a time to hold on and another to let go. In this life you have to do both. I want to keep love and freedom together in my heart."

I hold my side where Angie hit me and feel the beating of my heart in my hand.

Chapter 15

It's almost lunchtime when I get up. I look at myself in the mirror in the bedroom, and I see my frozen face, lime colored and pale.

Before I went to bed last night, long after midnight, I looked out the living room window at our block. The Foxy Lady was parked and locked, slumbering in peace. A light was on at Angie's, and it shone through the worn spots in the living room drapes. I wondered if that meant Char was awake or passed out. Before I dropped off to sleep, I thought about Angie's horse and flames painting and understood why she gave it to me. It was a smoke signal. A big SOS.

I walk slowly into the kitchen. Daddy looks up from the radio he was tuning to lake weather. I remember with a pang how stricken both Daddy and Ma were when we finally got home.

Daddy invites me to walk with him to the lake. I bump into him a little as we step down onto the sidewalk from our stoop. He tells me he doesn't want to walk past the picket line, which is the shorter way to the lake. My flip-flops are completely worn thin, and even though my side is sore as I walk, it is pain already tempered by familiarity. Soon enough I'll be throwing my flip-flops away and wearing shoes. I comfort myself by thinking high school will be starting soon. All that's happened will be drowned in the new routine of another season.

Daddy says he still can't get over the weather up here, how even in summer it can be cold and foggy. I look at my daddy walking, and even though the sidewalk is uneven, he seems to glide.

The route to the lake leads us toward the factory that makes floor and car waxes. We come upon the Golden Rondelle. I have seen this thing plenty of times on brighter days, passing by it in the car. Every time we go by, I say I want to go inside it, but we never stop. Today it is locked and empty.

We walk around the edge, feeling a little jumpy about what might pop out because of the gloom. I expect little green men to come out of it and kind of hope that happens. Daddy tries to touch its belly as we walk under it.

"Someday we should come over here and get a proper tour," Daddy says. I know that will never happen. We're not a family that plans things.

Across the street from the Golden Rondelle is the Dairy Queen where we had ice cream the day we went to the beach as a family after we moved to Rubberville, the day it seemed possible Daddy could do anything.

Daddy jingles the change in his pocket. I know he'd like to stop and get something. I can practically taste a Dilly Bar too. We keep going.

Daddy says, "Four solid blocks and not a stitch of grass. A smart guy would land his pretty flying saucer somewhere else."

As soon as we're past the Golden Rondelle and the DQ, the neighborhood changes into another world entirely. When we hit Wisconsin Avenue, Daddy says he knows the way to this beach that's private. The street itself is brick from the old days, and when a car drives on it, you hear rubbery, rumbling sounds. We turn and walk down Wisconsin Avenue toward the water. Daddy puts his arm around my shoulder for a minute while he decides which way to go. His arm feels light on my bare shoulders, nothing like Danny Simon's heavy arm the day me and Angie said good-bye to the ponies.

The houses on this street are big, mansiony. A few have columns and long driveways to the front doors. Those are the ones on the lake side. The air is heavier now that we're closer to the lake, and from somewhere a foghorn makes a regular moan. I think of all the floating vessels out there in the water. I smell fish and hear gulls too. Everything here passes on its way somewhere.

Me and Daddy look around the neighborhood, knowing Ma could be in any one of these places right now. We both look out for the station wagon but see no sign of it. One of the places we pass is lower to the ground than a regular house, with a flat roof. It's got big windows in front, taking in the view. Daddy says there are lots of houses like this scattered in this state. It's made by some famous architect who was against closets and basements. I don't really like the looks of it. I tell Daddy someday I'm going to live in a place like the one across the street. Servants will wait on me hand and foot. Daddy laughs.

At the end of the block we get to a white house that's up on the rocky hill. It's not so perfect as the other ones, no grand front door or shiny doorknobs. But it's big with rows of windows in the back that look out over the lake. The place seems to smile. There are no stupid yard decorations of any sort or wobbly trees. Just flowers, a picket fence, and weathered rocks. If the house could talk, it would tell me how much it likes being right where it is, and it looks like it has been there for a hundred years. It has green shutters anchored down against the wind coming off the lake. "Just try tearing me apart," the house says.

Daddy says that on the other side of the house is the trail that leads down to a private beach. It's been worn by many feet, and the dirt is packed down good. We walk it single file. It's not a beach, just a small strip of rocky sand and boulders that keep the waves from eating away the shore and the house. We go in search of something halfway flat to sit on. I climb over the rocks, careful not to slip or jam my foot. The waves are hitting the rock barrier, but there are still dry spots. I'm a little chilled but not too bad. The water makes a thunk as it splashes back into itself. The sound seems to come from deep in the earth, way below the lake.

Along the way Daddy picks up some rocks. He throws a couple in, and we hear that thunk some more. He gives me one, a chunk of glorified gravel. I stand up, and I whip it as hard as I can. I'm hoping to throw away loneliness and the heavy feeling in my heart. I almost lose my balance and hear a very healthy splash. Daddy says, "Careful there. Last thing we need is you falling in the lake." He motions for me to sit down with him.

I sit down and see a few things floating near the edge of the rock we're sitting on—a stray bobber, cigarette butts. I wish people wouldn't do that. I once saw a billboard that said, GIVE A HOOT, DON'T POLLUTE. I love Woodsy Owl.

"This strike has been such a killer," Daddy says. "I can't tell you how many miles I've logged on that damn picket line. . . . And your mother, working like a dog."

I ask him, "Have you thought about getting out of here?"

He turns his head and laughs a bitter chuckle. "Every day, child. Every day."

He coughs a little. The lines in his forehead wrinkle, proving to me that he knows what I really think, and it matters to him.

Daddy says, "Sometimes I look at that water and think about how cold it is and what it must be like if you got into trouble out there." This summer we heard about a guy who went out on the lake in a canoe despite the small-craft advisory. He must have wanted to die. He went out on the cold, choppy water with no life jacket, no beer, no fishing tackle, none of the usual clues that he intended to return to shore alive.

Daddy's face gets tighter as he squints into the misty air. "But then I think about how beautiful it could be, surrounded by nothing but water. That all you could see would be blue—waves and sky—and feel lighter than air."

I feel weighed by all the things that have gotten worse this summer. The strike is down for the count. I made and lost my only best friend.

The idea of swimming still unsettles me, but every time I come to the lake, I feel a little less afraid. As Daddy predicted, I've gotten to know the lake better. He lights up a cigarette. "I'd really like to take a boat out someday," he says.

I nod. The idea seems really farfetched. Even when we had the worms and fishermen asked him to go with them, he always said he'd stick to fishing from the shore. You could catch all the fish you'd ever need right from the water's edge, he insisted.

We look out into the misty lake together and listen to the foghorn. There are things out there we won't ever see.

We sit like birds on the rocks, facing the wind, watchful. I look at the choppy waves, the blue-black depths, feel the chill coming off the water. Daddy says, "I never remember to bring an extra shirt when I come out here." That's the truth. We rub our hands over our upper arms to ward off the chilliness.

"Are we gonna move again?" I ask. I know the strike isn't going well, that Daddy's harbored thoughts of moving on. I've been thinking it too. Leaving Angie and Rubberville behind would probably be a good thing.

"Well, there's been talk of getting back to work. Some guys are saying a crappy job is better than none," Daddy says. He bows his head. "Sometimes things happen during strikes, people end up . . . you just never know." I remember the night all the men came over to talk about fairness, how Daddy seemed so energetic, as if this time he could make a difference.

"Sure," I say. I recollect Rita's question to me: If you were on your deathbed, what would you be most proud of? I still don't have an answer.

"But I don't know. We'll see what happens. I just don't want you to be surprised. Okay?" He coughs a little again. I'm still waiting for the we're-moving-on-to-a-better-place speech.

We each throw in a little rock as if it were the period at the end of a long sentence.

"Libby, some things you just want to do over and over again to make them right. But sometimes you really only ever get one chance."

"Have you ever done anything you wish you could do over?"

He turns away from me and fumbles to light another cigarette. His hands tremble as he gets his lighter's flame to meet the tip. Daddy inhales deeply on the cigarette.

"I built a raft once. I even had a pirate flag I made out of an old white undershirt, a skull and crossbones drawn on it with charcoal. I'll always remember it. I built that raft with my own hands."

I remind him he told me already.

He nods. "I showed it to my brother when I was done." He keeps going, repeating himself as if he hasn't heard me. "He was so impressed. And jealous. I made my older brother jealous." He smiles at the idea. "You know, Libby, that was probably the first and last time I've ever made anyone jealous."

"Did you say *older* brother? I didn't know you had a big brother."

"Yeah, Libby. I had an older brother." I shiver at the news. How could I have not known?

Daddy fiddles with the lid of his cigarette lighter. I look for the spot where the lake meets the sky. The water looks milky. The waves that break against the rock we're sitting on are making a spitty foam that collects in a dip in the rock below us. I feel like we're in a room draped with a sheer curtain that clouds the view. I can still make out the shape of the house we passed on our way down here, though.

"Neither of us knew how to swim." Daddy stubs out his cigarette and puts his head down in the crook of his arm. He looks up, watery eyes and all. I look out at the water we're sitting by, water too rugged to see anything like ripples. I taste something like fish and metal in my mouth.

Daddy speaks as if he's in a trance. "He saved my life, but hardly on purpose, by going on that contraption first. When I knew he was in trouble, I ran. I heard a thousand heartbeats in my ears. That's what a soul sounds like when it's hanging on for dear life."

I breathe in time with Daddy. Daddy loves Lake Michigan, but when he gets close to it, I understand how he sees his older brother, the brother I never knew existed, who accidentally saved my father from drowning on the raft my father built with his own hands. Daddy closes his eyes as if he were floating, just as his brother surely did when he knew there was no turning back.

"Help came too late."

I see how my family has been shaped by this fact. Guilt washes over Daddy as naturally as water goes over rock. All his life he's been trying to make up for not being able to save his brother.

And I don't know how to swim. As much as Daddy's tried to persuade me to learn. Now I wish I weren't so afraid.

I feel waves crest and punch the boulder we're sitting on. My hands are still on the cool rock. The sky reflects nothing. The voice of the world is in the water.

"But there is one more thing," Daddy says.

Daddy stubs out his cigarette on the rock and, suddenly shy, looks at me. He tells me when he was in high school, he used to like a girl named Lily Jordan. Loved her. His telling me this surprises me, as if he had betrayed my mother before he knew her.

"She was real pretty, and she had an attitude that covered up how scared she really was." Lily lived with her daddy in the woods on a run-down farm. Her daddy pushed her around. There was no mama.

He asked her one day about that. She wouldn't say anything. He knew. He knew enough by that time to know that men sometimes did things to girls, took advantage of situations they shouldn't. I look at my daddy hard.

"One day Lily told me we had to quit pretending we had a future. She said, 'Let me go.'" And he did. He let her go.

Daddy tells me I'm different. Brave. Goodhearted. Angie might stand a chance now. He puts

192

his arms around me, and I smell fish and cigarettes.

"Libby," he says.

Daddy might not have been able to do anything for his brother or Lily, but he is here now.

"Daddy." I get a catch in my throat. "Me and Angie will never be friends again," I say. "Never."

And I start to cry.

Chapter 16

I have not even seen Angie since the day she hit me. Tomorrow we both start high school.

I surprise myself by calling her. She answers the phone right away. "Bring your bike and meet me by the tracks," I tell her. "Come with me to the beach," I say. "Bring your suit." She shocks me by agreeing.

I'm torn by hope and disbelief. When I get to the top of the tracks, she's not there.

I stand there like a toddler, fingers in my mouth, wondering where she could be and waiting. I blow on my fingers and feel feverish.

When Angie elbows me from behind, I'm so

relieved to see her. I want to hug her, but we don't touch.

I say what I've been waiting to say for a long time. I take a deep breath. "I'm sorry, Angie," I say.

Angie shrugs. "Well, Mom says good riddance now. We found out it's not the first time he's gone after somebody. Down in Florida was the last time, I guess."

"Really?" I think back to the day Kevin taught us about stabbing. I wonder if he taught the other girl that too.

"He was in prison before, and his name isn't even Kevin. It's William Meyer."

I wish I could brag and say I knew it, I just knew it.

Angie says he's in jail now, waiting to be sentenced. Hopefully, he will get a really long prison term. Again.

Angie tells me Char quit drinking and started cleaning the house. She doesn't want anyone to think she's unfit. But she's pissed at me especially, and Angie's not allowed see to me anymore. It occurs to me Angie's meeting me to defy her mother. It's my turn to shrug. I can't believe Char.

"I can't even think of him by his real name," I say. "He'll always be Kevin to me."

Angie sighs. "Me too. Now he's this big pervert, and I'm not supposed to miss him, but I do. I hate him, but I don't. He said I was the next Minnesota Fats."

I know what she means. He was the only grown-up who acted as if he cared about her future. But the person who truly believes in her is right next to her, not rotting in jail.

I think about the Snow-White and Rose-Red story and how the girls took pity on the dwarf when he was in trouble. But when Rose-Red could have left Snow-White in order to help the evil dwarf, she chose not to. I don't believe in happily ever after anymore, but I still believe in friendship.

Hope rises in my chest; my heart beats evenly. From here on out we could be better friends. It's possible. I feel generous again.

We get on our bikes and go. Cars pass us; a few boys hoot. I know they're not looking at me. Angie. Always Angie. We reach the lift bridge, the one that goes up and down for the barges and boats. No waiting right now. We look through the grates in the bridge and see the water below.

Our bike tires are soundless; my ears fill with the sound of zooms and the transitional crack back to the cement silence of the road. Angie's beach towel is tucked into her knapsack. We've got only one more big hill to go. We pass a sign: COOLER NEAR THE LAKE. Our town's new motto. We pedal past the city yacht club, pink stone, two stories, flying the flags of many countries, a green lawn the size of three football fields, nobody on it. There are cars parked in the lot, shiny, newer-looking. Not a soul out in this heat, though. Inside, having fancy drinks. Admiring boats. I recite the names of drinks I know because of Angie's mother—Manhattan, martini, whiskey sour—and ones I have tasted: brandy old-fashioned, gin and tonic, beer. Every last one of them sounds good right now.

Angie must be reading my mind. She puts her nose in the air and pedals her bike faster. I work myself hard, trying to keep up with her. Finally we get to the crest of the hill. It's downhill to the beach from here, and you can see it. The sand is almost white. I know it will be too hot to walk barefoot.

"Race you down!"

Angie pushes off, and I do the same. We're both tearing down the hill toward the beach and let fly. For the first time today I feel air cooling my skin, under my arms, around my ankles, brushing my forehead.

Oh, God, I've got the lead.

The road heaves. There's just no way to stop, so I head straight for the sand dune and hope for no broken bones. I hear Angie screaming, a big fake one, behind me. Heading toward the sand dune, I start screaming too. Whooping it up. Like old times. My bicycle tires get sucked into the mound of sand and stop. I let myself get thrown into the dune, the backs of my wrists plowing along four feet of hot sand. Angie does the same, and her front bike tire misses me by inches. Beach grass pokes me everywhere, and sand is sticking to places where I was sweating. I can't get up, and I can't stop laughing, burning up in this hot dune.

"Angie, didja see that? Holy crap. I thought I was gonna die."

"I thought you were too." She tries to get up and can't. We stay there, collapsed for a minute, on the dune.

"Oh, shit. I think I lost my quarters." She gets up on an elbow, spitting out the sand in her mouth. We both dig around our butts and the bikes. No luck.

A lifeguard's coming toward us, looking part watercolor in the heat waves.

"Uh-oh." We shrink a little into the dune.

"Afternoon, ladies."

Angie looks at me. We both think the same thing. He's so tan! His whole body. He reaches for our bikes.

"I'd like to point out the bike rack is over there by the concession stand."

"Yeah. We know. We just got here," Angie says.

"I heard. I'd also like to point out that the grass around these dunes is endangered." He points to other dunes with snow fences around them. "So I'll ask you to be more careful next time you bike down here."

"Hey, you know what?" Might as well ask while he's here, if he's going to act like a cop. "My friend here lost a bunch of quarters in the . . . accident. Can you help us look for them?" He reaches into the dune with hands as tan as the rest of him.

"Nope. Wait." He finds a quarter. It looks so

tarnished. It couldn't be one of those that Angie had. "Pick. Heads or tails." He flips it off his perfectly brown thumb, and Angie catches it in the air before it lands.

"Nice try," she says. You've never met a soul as ungrateful as Angie.

ANGIE HANDS ME a bottle of Hawaiian Tropic suntan oil. I smooth out my beach towel, trying to keep the sand off my newly oiled legs.

Before, we'd have spent half the day talking. Now we silently push sand around with our feet. My thin brown hair is in a single tight French braid Rita did for me, exposing the back of my neck. I can feel it start to burn.

I've been Rita's sister-improvement project since she and Frankie broke up. Rita admitted I was basically right about Frankie, and I felt close to her again, as if we had an understanding. I don't mind so much when she tells me I'd be much prettier if I just did my hair and put on makeup and dressed better and stood up straighter and smiled and quit acting like a baby all the time. It's Rita's way of making up for neglecting me this summer.

On the lake a freighter slides by, looking about the size of a caterpillar, and I hear the clap of waves slapping the lake. A horn warns from the lighthouse a mile away. It ends up inside my heart, joins a beat or two, and then makes its way out, like breath.

Down the beach a ways a man wearing mirrored aviator sunglasses is watching us. I watch Angie watch him. His mouth is curved in such a way, it's hard to tell if he's interested in her or thinks she's funny.

Angie cups a sticky hand to my ear and whispers, "He's cute." She sounds far away, as if I'm hearing her through a tin can connected by string.

"He's old," I tell her.

I look down at the sand. It is getting late in the afternoon. Our shadows appear to exchange looks, getting longer, more defined.

ANGIE SAYS SHE has something to show me. "I almost forgot; it's why I wanted to see you," she says, and she is excited for a moment.

She takes an envelope out of her backpack. "Mom had these printed."

Angie shows me the pictures of us from our pony

ride days at the sidewalk sale. She holds them gingerly, careful not to get Hawaiian Tropic suntan oil or sand on them. In the picture of me with Sally No I'm looking fiercely at the camera, my face taut, holding Sally No's reins in one hand. My other hand is on the pommel of the pony's saddle. I look every inch the hick Angie told me I was when we met. The me in that picture is someone who has not wised up. Angie is smiling in her picture; at least her lips are pulled back, her teeth dull bone as she hugs Not Sally around the neck. The only picture of the two of us has Danny in the middle.

I turn down Angie's offer to give me the picture of me and Sally No. "You keep it," I tell her. I'd be more grateful if I wasn't so sad about how things have turned out. I spent half my summer worshiping Angie and the other half agonizing over her. If we're going to be real friends, I don't need a picture.

I get up and go to the shore. I go in up to my ankles. The water is cold. Behind me are hills and trees, birds, a lighthouse, even a yacht club. Some sailboats skim the shallow areas, but mostly the yachts and ships are farther out. Little kids bob in the water at the shore. New moms help toddlers stand in the waves. I scan the water for the buoy that tells you how far out you should go.

I think about the strike; it just ended. Both sides "settled." According to Daddy, it wasn't a matter of anyone's winning. It was just over, and the strikers were guaranteed their jobs. They all took up where they left off, although a few scabs stayed on. Daddy said there was tension. All of them—management and workers—felt they had lost something when it was over. After almost a whole summer of Daddy's picketing on and off, and my seeing men standing on the sidewalk by Daddy's shop, the quiet seems deceptive, hiding the seething inside.

Now that Daddy's working again, Ma's been home more. She feels guilty that she didn't "see the signs sooner" about me and Angie and Rita. She is worried that I will be scarred for life by what I saw. When I talk to her about it, what I keep coming back to is Angie. Not speaking to her has been terrible. Ma thought it might not be a good idea to "reestablish contact," but she said she could understand my wanting to. She said she wouldn't stop me from trying to see Angie.

Could this be our last day together? I don't know

what will happen once school starts.

I sit down on the sand and start making a mound with the mucky sand at the water's edge. When we first moved here, that day at the beach, Toby and I built sand castles. "It's a way to start over," he said.

The sand at the shore is cold, wet, and fishy smelling. There's little driftwood pieces and tiny shells mixed in. A feather. Almost pretty.

"Angie, get over here," I demand. We have to build a sand castle.

I have big plans to build a fortress, with not one but two moats and a whole mess of towers.

Angie saunters over. "We need a bucket."

"No, we don't. Just use your imagination." I throw some of the mucky sand at her, and it splashes her legs.

"Libby, you're gonna get it now." Angie marches into the cold water and washes her legs. Water beads her upper thighs from the Hawaiian Tropic oil. Her skin is taut and pink. Neither of us will ever tan, no matter what we do.

Angie goes up to a child who looks to be about three years old. "I share with you," Angie says in kid language. "Bring back." She points to the bucket. He nods and doesn't cry when she takes his little shovel.

Angie uses the bucket and shovel for digging a hole near my castle. My towers are peaked, rimmed like melted candles.

"I'm gonna fill this thing up with water, its own little lake." She hauls bucket after bucket of water to the place she dug out. The water just seeps into the sand.

"I think it's hopeless, Angie," I tell her.

She starts to dig another hole. A very long, thin dish in the sand.

"Get in."

"No way."

"C'mon, I spent all this time doing this for you. It'll feel good. I guarantee it."

I give in. "Not a lot of sand."

"Okay, but you'll see."

I lie down in the area she dug for me. The sand is cool at my back. She uses the bucket and fills it with dry, hot sand from outside the hole she's dug. She pours the sand slowly over my knees. It does feel good, like a caress. She does this twice, three more times. With each bucket of sand I almost feel sleepy, as if I'm in a warm bath. I wait for each bucket. This is like being inside an hourglass, the sands of time dusting your arms and legs. She stops with the buckets, her chest rising and falling, breathing hard from all the work. My feet are completely covered with sand, the rest of me half. She sits down next to the cavity and starts pushing sand on me. It's the cooler stuff dug up from the bottom of the hole.

Angie says, "Someone buried me in sand once, and I liked it."

"Kevin?" I blurt.

Angie stands up and over me. "I'd shut up if I were you, Libby."

I feel sand fall lightly onto my chest; a few grains sprinkle my eyes.

"I should get out of here." I try to sit up.

I move my fingers and toes, but the sand holds my body down. I look up at the sky and hope not to be choked by sand. Angie carries over a bucket of water from the lake and threatens to splash my face with it.

Angie told me once about a tickle torture Kevin did to her and then demonstrated it by grabbing my arms behind me and tickling my stomach until I begged her to stop. As I lay heaving on the floor, she patted my head and told me I'd never make it.

I wouldn't be surprised if she tried something really mean to get even with me.

"Do you hate me?" I ask.

She puts the bucket of water down.

"Just wait." She straddles my torso and starts beating the sand on top of my stomach, patting it smooth. I feel the pressure of her beating hands, rubbing sand over my belly before she stands up. I feel her indecision, my bones asking to be saved by muscles that don't want to move. I think a gentle rocking might do it, and I begin the slow movements of toes and hands, expanding the sand. My fingers keep digging and digging.

From the neck down I'm completely crusted over. I must look like one of those sand candles. A swirl of wax poured in a hurry to form a misshapen blob. I'm always afraid of touching those things when I clean houses with Ma, in case the sand flakes off and makes a big mess on somebody's end table.

I stand up, bits of sand falling off in clumps.

I realize she covered me with sand head to toe so I'll have to wash off in the freezing-cold lake.

I'm not going to give her the satisfaction of letting

her know exactly how scared I am of the water.

The oceans of the world couldn't be this cold, but I go.

Past the knees and I just want to double over, but I keep going.

The part above the thighs, oh, oh, my God, the waist, worse.

The sand disperses with a little fizzing sound. My arms are stretched out; fingertips skim the water now, but still sand crusted. I feel the push and pull of the water. Finally the neck. I am practically numb.

Everything I have in my body is cold now: intestines, heart, liver even. But my head feels warm.

There's still sand in my ears. I put my head under and pull it out. Whoa.

The water makes my forehead ache, like when I eat an ice cream cone too fast. Not all my hair is wet, but enough.

In the lake up to my neck, I notice my body has a little float to it.

I bounce and let the water hold me. I start moving my legs and wonder, Does this movement mean I'm treading water?

I don't see Angie at the shore anymore. I'm not

surprised she ditched me, our friendship over.

Tomorrow I will sit in a class, clothed and dry. I'll smell new notebooks and desks and boy socks and lunchroom sandwiches and have a locker combination to memorize.

Will Angie boss me, slam my locker door, or ignore me? Will she talk about me to other people?

I'm sure I'm treading water the wrong way.

Daddy told me you tread water with your face down and pull it up for air and put it down in again. Breathe out. Arms out to the sides. Much better than trying to keep your head up.

I tread head up, puppy-dog style, moving in a straight line between the shore and buoy. If I make it to the buoy, I'll be fine. I try not to let myself panic even as I worry about being swept away. Drowned.

Of all the elements, I wonder, is water or fire the most destructive? I might be able to say if my teeth weren't chattering so hard.

I feel something on my thigh, and I should have known. Angie pops up from underwater, and I wonder where she got the guts to swim that far all the way under.

"See, Libby, you're going to be fine." Her face is

pure white, and her lips are blue. Her hair is slicked back on her head.

"You are crazy," I tell her.

She smiles.

She's dog-paddling too.

"Hey, look." She points toward the center of the lake.

I see nothing but water, a line of horizon. No matter how choppy the wave, that line always stays the same.

"I don't see anything."

"Follow me." She turns and bobs away out of reach."

I don't think I've ever felt so cold, my legs seeming to kick out against gravity itself as I try to keep up.

All I can see is my friend and the flick of deep waves cresting far away from us.

We kick away for every minute we are on this earth, letting the waves and the cold take the breath out of us.

We both grab the buoy, to catch our breath, to hang on to something besides each other.

Acknowledgments

I would like to express my profound gratitude to all the individuals and organizations that bless me with their time, talents, and resources. Thank you to the Minnesota State Arts Board and SASE: The Write Place for the financial support of their fellowships. Writing residencies at Norcroft, A Writing Retreat for Women, and the Ragdale Foundation gave me time to write and two Great Lakes to love. Steve Chandler and Ellen Doyle deserve thanks for graciously allowing me use of their studio space, as does Wendy Doyle for sharing her excellent photography skills.

The Loft Literary Center is my writing haven, and being a participant in the Loft's Mentor Series changed my life. I'd especially like to recognize Jerod Santek at the Loft Literary Center for his ongoing assistance.

Sandra Benitez and Robert Nixon have a knack for being there for me at crucial moments. I am humbled and grateful for their continual kindness.

Gail Graham, Mary Courteau, Kris Nelson, and Corinne Shindelar made it easy for me to have a day job. Their flexibility and understanding put me at ease.

I thank Maxine Clair, Holly Hee Won Coughlin, Liz Farr, Michelle Filkins, Scott Heim, Karen Hering, Milissa Link, Freda Marver, Sharon Roe, Martha Roth, Lori Stee, Pat Thompson, and Paula Yankee for their suggestions and encouragement.

My deepest appreciation goes to Paulette Bates Alden, Barrie Borich, Mary Logue, Alison McGhee, and Julie Schumacher for their excellent instruction and feedback.

I owe a huge debt of gratitude to my editors, Lindsey Alexander and Laura Geringer. Their editorial wisdom and enthusiasm for the book has been an amazing gift.

I could not have finished this project if not for the sustenance and camaraderie provided by the best literary posse in the Twin Cities: Carla Hagen, Alison Morse, Marcia Peck, and Julia Klatt Singer.

During the writing of this book, the hospitality of Cynthia Becker and Addi Ouadderrou kept me in good spirits. Betsy Sansby has been a confidante since the beginning, and provided me with many important breakthroughs throughout. Carol Indereiden has been all I could hope for in a soul sister—generous with her opinions, laughter, and friendship.

My parents, Jim and Nanette Cumbie, and my sisters, Peggy Creuziger and Elizabeth LaForge, are a bedrock of support and love. My brother, Jimmie Cumbie, has inspired me with his own dedication to the arts. My whole family has blessed me immeasurably.

Katze sat on my lap during the writing of this book and purred throughout two decades of my life. I'm grateful to have known such fierce loveliness. And, to my beloved husband, Sean Doyle, thank you for loving me through it all.